THE CHRISTMAS CASTLE

THE CHRISTMAS CASTLE

A HOLIDAY HOUSE NOVEL

J.L. JARVIS

BOOKBINDER PRESS

Published by Bookbinder Press
bookbinderpress.com

ISBN 978-1-942767-27-5 (trade paperback)
ISBN 978-1-942767-13-8 (paperback)
ISBN 978-1-942767-12-1 (ebook)

Edited by Red Adept Editing

To librarians, who have magic at their fingertips and know how to use it.

ONE

"I'm sorry, I can't accept that." Charlotte's face wrinkled up as the woman held out a zipped plastic bag that contained a children's picture book soaked in vomit.

"But it's a library book, and you're a librarian, so you have to take it."

Charlotte's face must have gone blank, because her mind nearly did. "I'm sorry, but we can't shelve that."

The woman's mouth widened, but no one would call it a smile. "I don't really care what you do with it."

"Mommy?"

Charlotte looked over the edge of the counter, where a preschooler tugged on his mother's arm with reserved for the young.

"I'm returning it on time." The woman would not relent.

"Mommy!" Nor would the child.

The young mother's shiny cropped hair shook as she bent down. "Shh! You'll make us late for your strategy lesson."

Charlotte couldn't help herself. The words just slipped out in a soft whisper not meant to be heard. "Strategy lesson?" *How much strategy does a four-year-old need?* He seemed to be doing quite well on his own.

The mother stood and faced Charlotte with the full force of her disdain. "His chess lesson. He's very advanced. Now, would you mind if we finished up here? The nanny called in sick, and I really haven't got time for this."

"Yes, of course, but you'll need to pay for the damage."

The mom arched a brow without saying a word.

Charlotte lobbed back her most neutral stare. "So... if you'll give me your library card, I can look up the charges."

The woman lifted her chin and gave Charlotte an icy smile. "I'm not paying for that. I returned it on time, so I think we're done here." She dropped the bagged book on the counter.

Charlotte flinched, fearing the bag might burst open.

"C'mon, Wyatt." The woman turned, grabbed her

son's hand, and walked to the exit, leaving the echoing click of heels in her wake.

The children's room director came over and quietly asked, "Everything okay?"

Without looking up, Charlotte winced as she cleared the debris under the plastic away from the barcode so she could scan it. Then she typed while she answered. "Oh yeah. Everything's fine. She returned the book—albeit marinated in barf—so she didn't think she should have to pay for it."

The director suppressed a smile. "She can afford it. She once hosted a library fundraising event I attended. In her Upper East Side penthouse."

Charlotte paused long enough to look at her boss with a disbelieving stare before she returned to the computer. "I guess I'll just put a bill on her account. "Returned book in damaged condition: soaked in vomit." She carefully picked up the bag by the corner and gently set it down inside the wastebasket. Then she fished out a disinfecting wipe from the bottom drawer and wiped down the work area. "I'll just BleachBit this counter, and then I'll be off."

Her boss stood, arms folded, with a grin on her face. "Excellent work."

"Yeah, well, thanks to that master's degree. Although I must have been absent the day they covered literary emetics in library school."

"It's a graduate seminar course for archivists called Reflux Remediation."

Charlotte smirked, which drew a laugh from her boss, then went into the office to pack up for the day.

CHARLOTTE HAD an hour and a half to kill before meeting her boyfriend for dinner. Technically, they worked the same hours, but it seldom turned out that way. She used to feel like a slacker, but she'd come to realize that there was a world outside of her job, and she longed to discover it. Perhaps it was the nature of their respective careers. Garrett Thatcher loved his work as a stockbroker. It seemed to recharge him, while her work exhausted her. She respected what he did and the time it demanded, but she didn't enjoy being left on the sidelines. It didn't help that Garrett was the sun in his universe. That was part of the deal, although she'd never expressly agreed to it. On occasion, he allowed her to visit his world.

It hadn't always been like that. When they'd met during graduate school, they had been practically normal. They'd studied in adjacent study carrels and gone out on the weekends—when he had time. Maybe that was when Charlotte had learned not to rely upon Garrett. He had life organized in compartments, each with its priority. She was in there somewhere, filed under "extraneous," and she was okay with that. It wasn't as if she needed a man to fulfill her life. She had a career, and she'd worked hard to get to her current position—a children's librarian in the New York Public Library system. And she loved it. Well, most of it.

But Christmas was coming—her favorite time of the year. She loved walking along the New York streets with their glittering lights and shop windows.

She was walking to meet Garrett when she looked up from her musings to find a shop window with an old-fashioned train set making its way through a snowy landscape. Antique decorations and toys hung in seemingly no order above the toy train. With its hand-painted sign and holiday inventory, the shop looked like a transplant from Dickensian London. Charlotte hadn't seen the place before, even though she'd walked the same route twice a day for the last five years. But New York real estate prices were high, and shops came and went. Since the shop was Christmas-themed, Charlotte surmised that it must be a short-term rental for the holiday season. Checking her watch, she realized she still had an hour before she was due to meet Garrett. She could never get too much Christmas, so she went in.

The shelves overflowed with antiques and collectibles, all having something to do with the season.

Perhaps it was only the afternoon light that came in through the window beside it, but something caught Charlotte's eye, and she had to look closer. A small snow-globe ornament with a red ribbon tied to it was looped over a tree branch. She couldn't resist picking it up and holding it up to the sunlight while the snow gently fell on the castle inside. A Scottish flag waved on its pole at the top of the tower.

"I see you've found it."

Charlotte turned to find a lanky gentleman with gray hair and a beard setting down a box by the display window. He stood and peered at her with kind eyes. "We just got that in. I hung it up on the tree just a minute ago. It must be meant for you."

She smiled. "I'm not really in the market for a snow-globe ornament. I just stopped in to look around, really."

"Just $3.99, and it's yours." He lifted his eyebrows and gave her a knowing smile, as if she should appreciate what a bargain that was.

She stared at the snow globe. "I'll think about it." She and Garrett were leaving the next day for Scotland. Charlotte had always wanted to go, so Garrett—without knowing or caring how transparent he was—chose the following week to schedule a long-overdue trip together. After five years, he would do anything to avoid visiting her parents for the holidays, not that there was anything wrong with her parents. He simply had things he would rather be doing, like putting an ocean between them. So he'd arranged for the trip.

Well, in truth, his administrative assistant had done all the legwork. She'd outdone herself with this one. She had reserved a room for a week in a castle in the highlands of Scotland. Charlotte would definitely have to bring back something special for her. Maybe she would find an ornament like this with the actual castle. If they didn't have ornaments, she was sure they would have dozens of alternatives like scarves, tote bags, or bone-china teacups. Whatever they had, Garrett's assistant would get something special for giving Charlotte what promised to be the trip of her life.

She moved on to a display of scented candles then picked up an old picture book. As she gently turned the crumbling corners of the pages, a woman came in with what looked like her grandchild in tow. The boy went straight to the window. While he watched the train on its journey, the woman picked up the ornament Charlotte had looked at mere moments before. She held it suspended from its ribbon and smiled as it slowly spun. "How much is this? I don't see a price tag."

The shop owner glanced up from the shelf he was

straightening. "Oh, I'm sorry. Someone else is getting that."

The woman grew cross. "Oh? Well, you really shouldn't display things that you don't intend to sell."

The older gentleman took the comment in stride. "You're so right. My mistake. Here, I've got the perfect gift for you." He pulled an old book off the shelf with a Victorian illustration on the cover.

The woman's face lit up. "*A Child's Garden of Verses!* We had this exact book when I was a child. Look, Gabriel." The boy glanced at it then continued to play with the train. "I'll take it," she said as she pulled a reluctant Gabriel to the counter. She paid for the book and left, looking much happier than the whining child she'd taken away from the train set. The bell rang lightly as they left, and the shop door closed.

Charlotte turned to the shop owner. "I thought that ornament was for sale."

"It is."

"But—"

"People don't always know what's best for them. That's why we need gifts, so others can give it to them."

"But this isn't a gift."

"It could be."

Charlotte took another look at the ornament.

The old man grinned. "*Carpe diem.*"

Seize the day? Maybe it was the spirit of Christmas

that seized her, or pre-vacation excitement. Whatever it was, Charlotte pulled out her wallet and bought the castle ornament. She could hang it over a bottle of champagne for Garrett when he joined her in the restaurant. What a nice way to kick off their trip. As the shop owner wrapped up the ornament, Charlotte said, "You're very good at what you do."

With a twinkle in his eye, the man said, "I get that a lot."

She took the wrapped package he handed her. "Thank you."

"You're welcome. Merry Christmas."

"Merry Christmas." Charlotte left the shop and walked down the street toward the restaurant with fresh holiday cheer. She glanced at her watch and saw that she was still a bit early. But she went to the restaurant and sat at a table by the window, content to watch life passing by while she waited for Garrett.

Charlotte sat alone at a table for two, her thick mass of chin-length auburn curls spiraling and bobbing as she talked on her phone with her friend Jen. "I'm just waiting for Garrett. No, I'm a little early." She glanced at her watch. It was 7:40. Well, she would've been early for an eight o'clock date. Unfortunately, theirs had been scheduled for seven. They were supposed to meet right after work, which for her was 5:30. She'd planned to work later to kill time before dinner, but the barf book had finished her off for the day.

"So what's the occasion?" Jen asked.

"Celebrating the start of our vacation. We're leaving tomorrow for Scotland."

"Oh, wow! That's tomorrow? But won't it be cold?"

"It's about like here."

"Right. So, cold."

"A winter wonderland? Yes. My thought exactly."

"How nice. And sudden."

Charlotte shrugged. "I know. It was Garrett's idea. I'm pretty sure he did it to avoid Christmas with my parents."

"You're going to miss Christmas?"

"No, I made sure that we're flying back on the twenty-third."

"Oh, okay. Well, it sounds very romantic!"

Charlotte's eyebrows drew together. "Yeah, it does, doesn't it?" More romantic than sitting all alone waiting for him.

"Oh, there's my doorbell," Jen said. "I ordered Chinese. Gotta go. But we'll talk before you leave. Bye."

"Okay, bye." Charlotte set down the

phone, and her smile faded. She'd done her best to sound cheerful with Jen, but the truth was she'd spent more time waiting on Garrett than dating him. She was forever waiting for dinner, waiting for phone calls, waiting five years for something to happen—like a relationship or, God forbid, a commitment. In his mind, they had one because she was usually—well, always—there for him. If he wasn't always there for her, then she managed without him.

Charlotte looked away as the host eyed her table. She was lucky they'd even seated her without the rest of her party. The restaurant was filling up. She flagged down the waiter and ordered another glass of wine. She and Garrett were regulars, so the server had waited on them before. "If you need the table, I can go to the bar and eat there."

He cast a sideways glance toward the door. "Sit tight. There's no wait list yet."

"Really, it's okay."

He gave his head a subtle shake. "Let's give it a couple of minutes. I'll go get you that wine."

A few tables away, a movement caught her eye. A young man got down on one knee and lifted adoring eyes to his date. With a jealousy-induced wince, Charlotte muttered, "Please be protesting the national anthem." But he pulled a small box from his pocket, and the elated young woman's hands flew to her face while the tears trailed down her apparently waterproof makeup. Charlotte had to admire a girl who was prepared for any contingency. The couple embraced, and the whole restaurant burst into applause. An unexpected tear clung to Charlotte's lashes.

"Nice! I don't usually get applause." Garrett slipped into his seat with a grin. The waiter arrived, and Garrett ordered a beer.

When the waiter was out of earshot, Charlotte stole a glance at her watch. "Is everything okay?"

"Oh yeah. I went out for a drink with some of the guys after work."

Charlotte's eyes widened. "You were at a bar with some guys? But I've been here waiting."

Garrett rolled his eyes and leaned back in his chair. "Oh, c'mon. It's not like I could say no."

"Why not? We had plans." She did not want them to be that couple that argued in restaurants, but she couldn't hide her irritation.

He frowned. "Someone's a little bit cranky this evening."

"I've been here for an hour." Charlotte looked away and caught sight of the engaged couple. She couldn't help but wonder what that must have felt like. She knew what it looked like—happy. And that was not how she felt. "Cranky?" She shook her head.

Garrett had an icy gleam in his eye. "Did I say cranky? I meant to say bitchy."

Charlotte's jaw dropped.

Garrett leaned back in his chair and narrowed his eyes. "C'mon, babe, you're ruining our holiday buzz."

"Your holiday buzz," she said softly.

He reached over and put his hand on hers. "Look, I'm here now, and we're going on vacation—no work, no family—just us!" He grinned with his even white teeth. "Let's not ruin it."

With a defeated sigh, Charlotte nodded—not because she could be so easily swayed, but because she didn't want the conflict. She was tired of it all—the excuses, the arrogance, and the overall lack of respect for her feelings and thoughts. So, the evening proceeded like it normally did, with Garrett talking about his day at the office. She, too, had been working all day, but she didn't have the energy to convince him to care about how her day had gone. She wasn't sure he would know how to anyway. She would deal with that steep learning curve later.

After they made it through dinner, they paid the check and headed for the exit. The engaged couple managed to get there before them, looking all full of joy as they walked outside to embark on their new life together.

Charlotte watched them disappear into the night.

"Garrett, do you ever wonder where you'll be in a year, maybe two?"

He took out his phone and checked the screen. "Hmm? Oh, New York."

She wrinkled her face. "That's not quite what I meant. I mean us."

He glanced up from his phone. "Well, unless you're moving, New York for you too."

Maybe she shouldn't have had that third glass of wine, because something snapped. But she kept telling herself not to argue as they silently walked the last block to her apartment.

"Charlotte? Is something wrong?" Garrett peered at her as though he were truly concerned. That was new.

She regarded the man whom she'd spent the last five years of her life with... sort of. "Wrong?" Then it just hit her. She knew what she had to do, and the weight of five years' worth of emotional baggage lifted from her shoulders as strains of an angelic choir echoed above. Or maybe someone was playing Christmas carols with their window open to compensate for the typically overheated New York City apartment. In any event, she felt almost giddy. "No, nothing's wrong. In fact, everything's right. More than right."

For once, she had Garrett's attention. He looked practically worried.

"Garrett, you never asked me where I see myself in the future."

He shook his head and shrugged.

Have I actually rendered him speechless? She ignored his apparent confusion. "Well, two minutes from now, I see myself on the other side of that door, without you. And a year from now? Same."

He opened his mouth, but she continued before he could speak. "I want you to be happy—just not with me. Goodbye, Garrett." She walked into the building and climbed the stairs to her apartment.

Once inside, her phone dinged with a text.

Garrett: *What about the trip?*

She deftly replied with her thumbs. *You can go without me.*

Garrett: *I'm not going alone.*

Charlotte: *It's okay.*

Garrett: *No, it's not! Why would I do that? It's insane.*

Charlotte: *Okay, well, I guess I could go.*

Garrett: *Oh. Okay, fine. Have fun on your romantic vacation—ALONE!*

She frowned at her phone before setting it and her bags down. There sat the box containing her new snow-globe ornament. She took it out and shook it. As snow swirled around the castle, her phone dinged again, but she ignored it.

"Maybe I will." The snow floated to the ground. "Well, why not? I'm a big girl. I can get on a plane by myself." She sank onto the nearest chair and tipped the snow globe again then leaned her head back and watched the snow gently fall on the castle inside.

TWO

JEN MANEUVERED through traffic on the way to the airport while Charlotte went through her checklist again. "Passport, ticket, credit card, backup credit card, money belt with emergency cash, lucky earrings, phone, and earbuds."

"Have you seen anyone about your obsessive-compulsive tendencies?"

The comment didn't faze Charlotte. "You mean my planning and organizational skills?"

"Yes, that." Jen kept her eyes on the road as she smirked. "What will you do with the other ticket?"

"There's nothing I can do but stretch out. Maybe sleep. It's an overnight flight. I'm not too proud to sprawl. Frankly, I can make use of that extra seventeen inches of seating with one thigh alone. I'll give those manspreaders a run for their money."

Jen grinned. "Sounds like a plan. Oh—help me watch for this exit. I always miss it and wind up on a scenic drive through Newark." Just as she said it, the navigation voice told her to exit. Five minutes later, Jen pulled up to the curb of the departures entrance and released the trunk.

Charlotte hopped out and retrieved her suitcase. She shut the trunk and went around to lean in the window. "Thanks for the ride!"

Jen reached over and clutched Charlotte's hand. Behind them, someone honked their horn several times. Jen leaned out of the driver's side window. "Just a minute!" she hollered. "I'm busy yelling at you!" She growled then turned to Charlotte with a warm smile. "Have fun! If you meet a prince in that Christmas castle of yours, don't forget to check for available brothers and friends."

Charlotte grinned and gave her friend's hand a squeeze. "Will do! See you in a week!"

The waiting driver honked again. Jen turned and waved with a smile. "Bleeping bleephole," she said as she pulled onto the road.

Charlotte rolled her suitcase through the automatic doors and made her way to the check-in counter. As the agent at the counter handed Charlotte her ticket, the woman began giving directions to the fast-track security line and the lounge.

"The lounge?"

"Yes. It's included in your business-class fare."

"Oh. Thank you." Business class? She didn't know about that. Charlotte walked away feeling as if Christmas had already started. She'd been too busy packing to look at the ticket, relying instead on the admin's itinerary. *Well, thank you, Garrett.* Business class was nice. Not that he was, but she didn't mind his trust-fund-babyish penchant for comfort.

She breezed through security. The mood lighting was a nice touch. Then she found her way to the lounge and checked in. After pouring herself a champagne at the bar, she found a window seat and sat looking out at the taxiing planes. With a sigh, she thought of how romantic the setting might have been if she had a guy to share it with. Then she shook her head. No, she was not going to be a woman who couldn't enjoy life on her own. This was the beginning of freedom. She no longer had to adjust her life for someone else's convenience—someone who made no effort to do likewise for her. After five years of that, she was going to do what she wanted, when she wanted to do it. She unobtrusively lifted her glass in a toast to herself.

Feeling hungry, Charlotte wandered over to the restaurant portion of the lounge and enjoyed a leisurely buffet dinner. She had finished eating and was enjoying an after-dinner liqueur when they announced that her flight was ready for boarding. It felt different to walk past others who were waiting to board and go straight onto the plane. She should have felt guilty, but she couldn't lie to herself. It felt great. Why hadn't she ever done this before? Oh yeah, money. All the more reason to enjoy it.

She found her seat and got settled. A flight attendant appeared and offered to hang up her jacket. He returned with a glass of champagne. By the time another flight attendant made the rounds with amenity bags, followed by a second glass of champagne, Charlotte was settling into a new way of life.

A FLIGHT, a tram, a train, and a taxi ride later, Charlotte stood at the entrance of Craigthorn Castle, a stately stone castle perched on a cliff overlooking the sea, in the Highlands of Scotland. The fact that it resembled the castle in her snow-globe ornament did not escape her. The taxi driver carried her bags to the door then graciously declined the tip she offered, completely throwing her New York sensibilities off kilter. She thanked him profusely then simply stared at the castle, overwhelmed by its beauty and her jet-lagged condition.

A cheery young blond woman emerged from the entrance and gave Charlotte a warm welcome to Craigthorn Castle. She introduced herself as Ivy, and the earnest young man who followed her out was named Robby. He whisked Charlotte's bags inside, while Ivy took Charlotte on a brief tour through the tartan-carpeted halls, pointing out the breakfast and dining rooms, pub, and library, all available for guest use. The tour finished up at Charlotte's room.

She unlocked the door and walked in. Stone walls lined the room, and white linen curtains were tied back on the sides of the windows. Sun poured in through the uneven glass windowpanes, and the lamps on the nightstands gave the dark corners a comforting warmth. Curtains were tied to the corner posts of her grand four-poster bed. A blue-and-green tartan lay across the fluffy white duvet, while an inviting arrangement of pillows was propped at the head.

Resisting the urge to collapse on the spot, Charlotte thanked and tipped Ivy, who urged Charlotte to let her know if she needed anything. When Ivy closed the door, Charlotte went to the window across from the bed and gazed out at the sea. The old glass cast the landscape in soft focus. Dark clouds gathered off in the distance, but the sun still shone over the shore, where waves lashed the rocks. Craigthorn Castle, its grounds, and the rough coastal setting conjured a timeless, raw romance that Charlotte found irresistible. She couldn't imagine what had possessed Garrett to choose such a stunningly magical place to vacation.

She went to the other window of her corner room. When she saw that it overlooked a links golf course, her question was answered. Not even winter could quash Garrett's obsession with golf. It was his one passion in life. Charlotte sighed and stared at the links. With their wild grasses, deep bunkers, and irregular hills jutting up from the ground, even Scotland's golf courses projected an untamed spirit.

What better send-off for an unsatisfying relationship than to visit a place that embodied the polar opposite? Charlotte took a deep breath, braced by the staggering romance of the place—a romance Garrett would never know.

Looking back, she realized she had clung to her feelings for Garrett long past the time when she'd known their relationship wasn't enough. In a way, she'd been grieving the loss for the past several months and had only recently arrived at the stage of acceptance. This week would give her much-needed time to replenish her soul.

She looked back at the bed. Everything was perfect, but she was exhausted. After rearranging the pillows to make room to lie down, Charlotte collapsed on the bed for a quick power nap.

CHARLOTTE SAT STRAIGHT UP in bed and recalled where she was. She reached for her phone and saw that it was 2:30 a.m. This was why the common jet-lag advice was to resist the urge to sleep upon arrival. But Charlotte didn't do well without sleep, so she'd ignored the advice and decided that being awake hours before anyone else was better than a bout of sleep-deprivation-induced psychosis. She turned on the nightstand light and looked around. She could never go home if it meant leaving this place.

Twenty minutes later, she finished the espresso she'd made with the machine in her room and went to the library. She had dozens of books on her phone, but they weren't bound in leather and nested in centuries-old mahogany shelves, waiting to be discovered.

As she approached, she saw a fire blazing beneath a dark marble mantel. She hadn't expected a fire at such a late hour. Drawn to its warmth like a moth, she stood before it and looked up at shelf after shelf of books.

"Morning person or fellow insomniac?"

Charlotte flinched and turned toward the rich masculine voice to find a man shuffling papers into a file folder. She had walked right past him without even seeing him.

He rose from a wingback chair. "Sorry. I've startled you."

"I... didn't see you."

"I thought not. Didn't mean to lurk in the shadows." He grinned and reached out his hand. "Ian MacKay."

"Charlotte Glass." They shook hands. *That's a large, warm hand, Ian MacKay.* She shook off the thought.

Ian gestured toward the sofa beside his chair. "Have a seat." There was that hand again, large and beautifully formed. And the hand was attached to a sturdy arm and broad shoulders.

They sat down, he in the regal wingback chair and she in the tufted leather sofa that faced the fire. It was so unlike her to sit down with a stranger. Although she'd grown skilled at concealing her shyness, she had never completely overcome it. Ordinarily, she would have made an excuse and departed posthaste. Maybe it was his soft Scottish accent. But there she was in a castle, chatting with a strange man. Actually, strange was not quite the word anyone would use to describe Ian MacKay. Despite being a serial name forgetter, she remembered his name, which was the least memorable thing about him. From her new seated perspective, she noticed how the light fell on the strong planes of his face, the full lips, and the gentle gray eyes that seemed exceedingly focused on her.

"I wasn't expecting to find anyone else up at this hour," Charlotte said. "But to answer your question, it's jet lag. I'm definitely not a morning person."

He nodded in approval. "Good. I could never be friends with a morning person. Not that there's anything wrong with the lot, but I tend to resent them."

Charlotte's eyes brightened. "Exactly. It's unnatural."

He shook his head. "Springing out of bed all bright-eyed? Intolerable. It's enough to make one want to..."

"Climb back into bed." As they shared a laugh, Charlotte made a mental note to change the subject to something other than climbing back into bed. It might make her mind wander. Caught up in the joy of Ian's quick sense of humor, she leaned forward and said, "I've dumped men for less." Her smile instantly faded as she recalled that she had indeed just dumped a man, although for a far better reason.

"Recently?" Ian apparently didn't miss a thing.

Charlotte was a terrible liar. She'd learned the hard way that it was futile to try. Ian was waiting attentively, so she blurted it out. "Yesterday—or the day before, I guess, with the time change. I haven't slept, and we're...

how many hours ahead? Anyway, I feel like I've lost a day, and—" She stopped. "I'm rambling."

"Sorry—about the breakup, that is. Although on behalf of the Royal Greenwich Observatory, I apologize for the time change as well." He didn't look at all sorry about any of it.

Suddenly, neither was she. "It's okay. It needed to happen. It was one of those things you put off, but you feel better after it's done, kind of like filing your taxes." She made a futile effort to smile.

That drew an intrigued look with a hint of amusement from Ian.

Charlotte tried to recover. "So how about you? Dumped anyone lately?"

His embarrassed grin was too endearing. "No, I'm afraid not."

Does that mean he has somebody he wishes he had dumped? "Well, good. I'm sure Mrs. MacKay will be happy to hear it." She forced the "how nice" smile she'd perfected while working with the public.

"Mrs. MacKay is my mother. Was, actually."

"Oh, I'm sorry."

"Thank you. It's been years. I'm surprised I even mentioned it." He glanced away for a moment then back at Charlotte. "What I mean is, there's no other Mrs. MacKay, at least not in my family." He smiled.

"Oh." Charlotte tried not to appear too relieved.

"No. I almost married once, but... I think she remembered that she had some taxes to file." A glimmer came into his eyes.

"Oh, sorry." Charlotte tried to look sorry.

He shrugged. "It was a long time—well, months ago. As you see, I've recovered. I'm fine."

She could not agree more. He looked fine to her.

He studied her. "So... you're American?"

She nodded. "Worse. A New Yorker."

"But that's brilliant!"

"Is it?"

He leaned toward her enthusiastically. "Och, what a city! So much energy."

"Well, I can't deny that. And I suppose you're from—"

"Here." They both said it at the same time and grinned.

Charlotte's gaze swept over the room. "This seems like a wonderful place to be from."

His eyes softened. "It is that," he said quietly. As a comfortable silence settled between them, he abruptly stood and scooped up his file folder.

He was tall and strapping. Charlotte had begun to guess his height earlier, but his broad shoulders had distracted her. She now thought he might be about six-two, maybe six-three, a good half foot taller than she was.

"Well, I'll leave you to enjoy the library," he said. "Please feel free to borrow any book that interests you."

Charlotte was stunned. "But some of these must be..."

He looked straight into her eyes. "Old? Yes, they are."

Charlotte nearly forgot what they were talking about. His gaze had some serious wattage. Maybe in the Highlands, they'd developed some sort of mutation that sucked the good sense out of smart girls through their eyes. Although with Ian, losing her mind might be a small price to pay.

"You're welcome to them."

She blinked. "I'm sorry, I..." *Welcome to what?* With his beautiful eyes, it was a wonder any girl could maintain her thoughts or balance around him.

"The books. Help yourself." He smiled, although his mouth had a crooked, amused angle to it that made her a little self-conscious.

Somehow, she recovered. "Oh, I couldn't. I mean, some of these volumes shouldn't even be touched without white gloves. I'm sure the owners wouldn't want me to—"

"I'm sure he would." He seemed awfully confident. "Besides, the really valuable ones are locked in glass cases."

Charlotte eyed him with reluctance, but her temptation was gaining ground.

He leaned toward her. "Books are meant to be read. Otherwise, they're just valueless bundles of paper." He offered his hand. "Enjoy your stay, Charlotte."

She shook his magnificent hand and might have held on if he hadn't slipped it from her grasp, turned, and left.

What had just happened?

I'll tell you what just happened. A good-looking man just appeared in the castle library and chatted you up like you've never been chatted before. And no, you don't smoke, so you can't have a cigarette.

She sank into the leather sofa. Of course, it wasn't love at first sight, mainly because that didn't happen. And really, he hadn't had her undivided attention until he'd said what he had about books. Until then, he'd just been another ruggedly good-looking man with a rich voice and an accent too charming for anyone's good. No, what she felt was not instant love. It had taken at least a few minutes before his vigorous manliness had reached into her heart... and her soul... and perhaps other places.

Charlotte rolled her eyes and winced. This was not like her. She had never met a man and had feelings like this. It had to be the jet lag. Sure, she might have felt an attraction, but that was only because Ian had the sort of looks that would attract any woman with a detectable pulse and a properly functioning limbic system. It wasn't fate. They were not meant to be. It was no more than chemistry—pheromones—God's little way of ensuring the species would not go extinct. Apparently, the Almighty was determined to keep this guy's bloodline going.

She gazed at the fire's amber glow. The Highlands of Scotland were a mystical place. *Who knows? Outside at this very minute, a zombie apocalypse might be underway.* And if luck would have it that she and Ian were the last two survivors on earth, well, what choice would they have? Someone would have to repopulate the planet.

She would take one for the team.

THREE

CHARLOTTE WENT DOWN to the breakfast room, where a fire crackled in the large fireplace. Half a dozen couples sat scattered about, quietly sipping their coffee or tea and enjoying their breakfasts. Between the jet lag and guilt over her uncanny rebounding ability, she hadn't slept well. She'd finally concluded that she had spent the last five years getting over Garrett, so by the time she finally let go of any hope for a happy future with him, the heavy lifting was done. With that settled, she'd promptly fallen asleep. For three hours. And so there she was, ready to face a new day... with the aid of some coffee.

She glanced about for a table, as well as for Ian, which was not part of the plan. She'd worked it all out first thing that morning and had convinced herself that, beyond pleasant hellos, it would be best to ignore him. If only he were there to ignore.

She sighed and gazed at the assortment of paintings adorning the room—originals, no doubt. The place was a living museum. Garrett had chosen well. The castle could not have been a more perfect winter escape, a lucky mistake on his part. Looking around, she saw only middle- and older-aged couples. And then there was twenty-seven-year-old Charlotte. In the week before Christmas, of course it made sense that the only people she would find there would be those with no shopping or family visits to attend to, people with the freedom to travel.

Charlotte had freedom to travel, at least for the week, and freedom from everything else. She still felt a bit guilty about taking the trip—not that Garrett would have come by himself. Still, he couldn't have gotten a refund at such a late date, so he was out the money either way. But for him, it was chump change. He'd lost more in a day on the stock market than the trip cost. He would be fine. And she had paid him back for her share of the trip. He'd originally meant for it to be his Christmas present to her. Of course he'd also meant for himself to be part of the gift. *Figures.* If he wasn't God's gift to women, he could at least be God's gift to her.

That was why gift receipts were invented.

A linen-textured card lay on the table with

suggestions of things to do for the day. Golf, hunting, and fishing were not at the top of her list. As much as she might have enjoyed a drive through the area, she was terrified by the prospect of driving on the left side of the road. She was sure she would wind up looking the wrong way at an intersection, and that wouldn't end well. She wondered if Garrett had thought about driving. He could have, but only if it served his purposes.

Her musings were interrupted by the arrival of a full Scottish breakfast of eggs, bacon, beans, one stewed tomato, potatoes, mushrooms, black pudding, and a thick slice of homemade brown bread. Charlotte might not have known when to sleep, but her appetite was well up to the task of breakfast regardless of what time it was in New York. So much so, that she thought she'd best go walk it off after she ate.

A leisurely half hour later, she emerged from Craigthorn with a map she'd found in her room. Several paths led away from the castle. She chose one that appeared on the map to lead to a cliff that jutted out from the shoreline. The chilly sea air blew against her as she watched the wild waves assault the rocks and wash onto the low-lying shore. Gulls swooped down and soared overhead while Charlotte carefully worked her way along the narrow path that led down to the stony beach.

There were days in New York when she felt so alone in the midst of the crowded Midtown sidewalks, but here she was truly alone yet felt wholly content. As far as she could see in any direction, there wasn't a soul to disturb her solitude. Not even the castle was visible from her current spot. In the hundreds of years since Craigthorn had been built, it couldn't have changed all that much. Even as the vastness of life and the world seemed to hang in a tenuous balance about her, being there felt simple and good for her soul.

The light dimmed as thick clouds rolled in from the sea, and a mist moistened her face. Moments later, a drop fell, then another. She turned and started back for the castle. By the time she arrived, the freezing rain had turned to snow, but not before she was drenched. She took her coat off and shook it outside before going in. Then she wiped off her shoes and made sure to dry them enough to spare the tartan carpet she'd so admired the previous day.

It seemed like an opportune time to take Ian up on his offer to borrow a book. So she returned to her room, changed into dry clothes, and headed for the library in search of a book and an undisturbed corner.

Two couples sat in front of the fire. They all exchanged polite introductions and a few words about the weather, then Charlotte turned her attention to books. By the time the couples had gone, she had

Walter Scott's *The Bride of Lammermoor* in hand and was curled up in a window seat, lost in Ravenswood Castle while the flickering fire warmed the room.

TAKING A BREAK FROM HER READING, Charlotte wandered down for some lunch. She sat by the window, which was drizzled with rain, and enjoyed a hot bowl of Cullen skink and a salad topped with salmon strips. She could almost hear Garrett chastising her for ordering fish. He couldn't stand to smell it on her breath. She smiled and dipped her spoon back into the bowl of thick Cullen skink. She almost wished he were there, if only to witness her act of rebellion.

The sun made an unexpected appearance. The weather must have blown over, which meant she could go out and finish the walk she'd missed out on earlier. She glanced about the thinning dining room. Meals were served within narrow windows of time, so she wondered how she had managed to miss Ian MacKay yet again. But then she realized that he must work there. Why else would he have been in the library in the middle of the night? So he was probably working somewhere out of sight. She might not even see him again. She sighed then felt foolish and banished further thoughts of Ian MacKay from her mind.

Once outside, she chose a different path that led away from the cliff and the beach, afraid portions of her earlier path might be slippery after the rain. At the last minute, she'd left her hiking shoes at home to make space in her carry-on luggage. Now she regretted that choice. The first stretch of the path bordered the golf course, where one stalwart golfer was playing on the snow-dusted course. That was some dedication, and Garrett would've been right out there with him. Although there she was out walking in the same cold, damp weather, so she really didn't have reason to judge.

The sun gave up its earlier attempts to shed light and warmth, but the brooding gray clouds cast their own brand of beauty in uneven shadows spread over the cliffs and the grasses bent with frost. If ever there were a place to retreat to one's thoughts, this was it.

Charlotte was alone in the world.

She finished walking off any lingering effects of her jet lag and returned to the castle clearheaded. Once inside, she turned to head up the stairs to her room, when Ian rounded the corner and nearly ran into her.

He grasped her shoulders to keep from colliding. "Sorry! Close call." He grinned with a hint of mischief in his eyes. But when their eyes met, his smile faded, and they froze for a moment. He removed his hands from her shoulders and politely inquired, "Did you enjoy your walk?"

"Yes." A sudden realization struck her. "Was that you playing golf?" Although the golfer had been too far away for her to see his facial features, the clothes looked the same.

"Aye. I saw a wee window to fit in a few holes, so I took it." He grinned, color still in his cheeks from the brisk outdoor air.

Charlotte nodded. *Fantastic. Another golfer.* If Garrett had come along, they would have wound up best friends. *Lovely. Scratch him off the list.* Not that she had a list—or that he would have been on it. She glanced at the stairway. "Well, enjoy your day." With a smile, she started up the stairs.

"I'm sure I will." He climbed each step of the wide, curving staircase beside her. They arrived at the top and faced each other.

Charlotte smiled again. "Well, see you around."

He stood there for no more than a second or two, but it was long enough to feel awkward. Charlotte tried to sidestep her way around him, but her shoe caught in the carpet and launched her into a fall. As she reflexively flailed her arms, Ian pulled her back onto her feet and into his arms. Once securely planted, she loosened her death grip on his biceps. He let go of her waist.

"I guess this is the part where somebody says we've got to stop meeting like this," Charlotte said.

His eyes twinkled. "Assuming one wanted to stop."

Charlotte took a step back. "Yes, well, thank you."

"Anytime, Miss Glass."

"Charlotte," she corrected with a modest roll of her eyes.

"Charlotte," he said with a nod. "You may still call me Mr. MacKay."

That broke the spell. Her eyebrows furrowed as she opened her mouth to protest.

His lips spread to a smile. "I'm sorry. Call me Ian. For some reason, when I'm with you, I find myself wanting to laugh."

She grimaced. "Thank you?"

He reached out and lightly brushed his hand down her shoulder. From anyone else, it might have been a gesture of kind reassurance. From him, it was like a match on the side of a matchbox. She blushed.

Not seeming to notice, he squinted and peered closer. "I've got just the thing for us. Come with me. That is, if you wouldn't mind."

Charlotte did not even try to hide her confusion. "That depends."

"Upon what?"

"On whether you're going to tilt a wall sconce and

take me down some hidden passage to my ultimate doom."

He looked pleased. "Actually, you're not too far off."

"Oh. Gosh, look at the time. This is when I usually clean the sock lint from my toes." She turned to leave, but he caught hold of her hand. In addition to a gaze that made her heart pound, Ian had hands with the power to stop her in her tracks—kind of like tasers but with none of the pain. Yeah, those arms were stun guns.

"Charlotte, relax. I was joking. It's in the library."

"What is?"

"My surprise." He looked into her eyes. "You're perfectly safe. If it makes you feel better, all the hallways have CCTV."

She stared blankly at him.

"Sorry. Closed-circuit television. It's monitored twenty-four, seven by the security staff."

Charlotte frowned. "Oh, great. So by now, they've got that fall of mine on a loop and are uploading it to social media. Wait. How do you know so much about the security equipment and procedures? Are you some sort of cat burglar casing the joint?"

He slumped his shoulders. "Sadly, nothing nearly as exciting. I'm the owner."

"Of the security system?"

He smiled and seemed almost embarrassed. "Well, that, and this." He lifted his palms in a gesture that made it all clear.

"Of all this? You mean the castle?"

He winced. "I'm afraid so."

"Oh." She took a moment to let it sink in. "So does that make you the laird?"

"It does. Which means that—och, it's so anticlimactic now—but I know a place in the library where we can find some good whisky."

She gave him a deep, searching look. "Whisky? Well, why didn't you say that in the first place?"

"Aye, it might have saved us some time." He held out his crooked arm. "Madam?"

IAN PAUSED outside the library door. "I can only show you if the library's empty." He put his finger to his lips and opened the door a crack. He lifted an eyebrow and tilted his head. "All clear."

He walked to a corner near the window and ran his finger over the tops of some leather-bound volumes that turned out to be false book spines concealing a cupboard. "Here we are." He pulled out a bottle and a couple of glasses and set them down on the top of a cabinet. Ian poured and handed Charlotte one of the glasses. "*Slàinte mhath!*"

She repeated the phrase, and they drank. "I gathered that was a toast, but for all I know, it means "you ugly cow.""

He lowered his chin and lifted his eyes to meet hers. "If it did, I'd be terribly wrong. Actually, it's Gaelic for "good health.""

"Oh, good." Charlotte's eyes shone as she lifted her glass. "*Slàinte mhath* to you too."

Ian followed her eyes to the gray mist-covered coastline. "This a good place to be on a day like this—inside with a whisky in hand. Is it not?"

"Yes. It's perfect." She turned from the window to find Ian's gaze fixed on her. She froze, unable to form a coherent thought other than short, simple phrases like "gray eyes," "brown hair," and "can't breathe." Sipping whisky, which wasn't her usual beverage of choice, seemed to help—so long as she wasn't looking at him.

Look at you, Charlotte. Standing here, making googly eyes at the laird of the castle. She paused to let that thought settle. The laird of the castle. This was crazy. She didn't need a rebound guy... or laird. What she needed was—

"Supper?" His voice pulled her back from her thoughts, but her distracted state must have shown. "Have you got plans?"

"Just to eat at some point. Although I wouldn't actually call that a plan. More of a habit, really." She inwardly groaned. She was doing that thing she did, saying anything to fill in the space while she got over her nervousness. He didn't seem annoyed by it—yet—but he did have a confused sort of smirk on his face.

"So... would you care to eat at some point, preferably this evening, with me?"

"Oh." It was only dinner, yet it felt like the first step into something she wasn't quite sure she could manage. She was way too susceptible to his masculine charm for her own good.

"Nothing fancy," he added. "Just some pub grub in town. My treat."

The sensible thing would have been to make an excuse and stay on the safe side of the figurative line she was about to cross over. However, she couldn't help but find him charming, by which she meant wildly attractive. She reminded herself that she hadn't come to Scotland for this. Whatever this was.

She must have waited too long because he added a teasing inflection. "There's live music tonight, so you'll barely be able to hear me when I start to bore you." Charlotte's lips parted to answer, but Ian spoke first. "Och, I'm an eejit. You just broke up with your boyfriend. The last thing you need is some bloke pressuring you to go out."

"No, that's not it." *Yes, it is.* "I think it's... just jet lag." *How long can I use that excuse?*

He looked pleasantly surprised yet not thoroughly convinced. "If it is the ex-boyfriend, we could just pretend to be friends."

Her face wrinkled up. "Pretend to be friends?"

He smiled. "Yes. We've both got to eat. And you're fun to be with." His eyebrows drew together pitifully. "I can only hope that, in time, you might find me barely tolerable."

Why does he have to be so danged appealing? She would not succumb. She would use his favorite weapon, charm, against him. She smiled sweetly. "I already find you barely tolerable."

His face lit up. "Well, that's brilliant! Then we're on for this evening?"

Wait. That wasn't what she meant. How had he done that? He had undermined her defenses and won. And he'd managed to make her not mind. "Yeah, I guess so."

"Good." He got up and put the whisky back in its hiding place. "Let's meet downstairs tonight at, say, eight?"

Charlotte nodded. "Okay. See you then." She got up, smiled, and left. As she walked down the hall, she didn't know what to think, let alone feel. *Does he do this with all the guests? No, of course not—only the ones he finds attractive.* Did that mean he found her attractive? So what if he did? Smarmy rogues also found people attractive. Maybe they all used that "pretend to be friends" line. He might make a habit of preying on guests. But if that were the case, he would have bad online reviews from disgruntled women.

Pretend to be friends. What does that even mean? She went into her room and closed the door gently behind her.

It means you're in trouble.

FOUR

THAT EVENING, Charlotte went downstairs a few minutes early and found Ian in a chair near the door. He looked up, and she felt her smile bloom from within. "You're here."

He glanced at his watch. "Eight o'clock?"

"Yes, but—you're right. Eight o'clock." She'd grown so used to waiting for Garrett that she'd planned on her usual wait. She made a mental note: *It's time to let go. This isn't New York, and this definitely isn't Garrett.*

Ian led her to a weathered old Rover. "I hope this is okay. I've just sold my car, and this is it in the interim."

Charlotte wasn't sure why he sounded apologetic about it. Anyone she knew with a vehicle drove a car that was weathered and old, even if they were late models. Life was hard for a car on the mean streets of New York.

They pulled up and parked in front of a building that looked as though it hadn't changed in the last four or five hundred years. A cold wind tossed about the light dusting of snow.

As they walked into the pub, everyone Ian encountered greeted him with genuine warmth, which was another reason to cross "rogue" off the mental character profile she was forming. Charlotte slipped into a booth with a view of the fire, while Ian went to the bar to get them something to drink. She surveyed the dark, smoke-stained walls and beams decked with evergreen garlands and twinkle lights, and she felt oddly at home. Ian chatted with the bartender, while a small group of musicians gathered in the corner.

A woman tuned up her fiddle, while another played a few warm-up passages on the penny whistle. A young man pulled out a drum, which he held in his hand. By the time Ian returned with their drinks, Charlotte counted eight people seated in a circle, poised to play. As the music began, Charlotte's heart swelled. It wasn't only Christmas magic she felt. Yes, the magical place was cozy and warm, but what she felt most of all was content. For five years, she'd adjusted her words and her actions to keep the relationship with Garrett going. While she'd never felt trapped, it had too often been strained. She was startled by the ease she felt here, in this pub, with this man.

She lifted her eyes to find that Ian had returned and was studying her. He smiled and continued to gaze. Charlotte averted her eyes and watched the musicians.

"You like trad music, then?"

She turned back to him. "I don't really know. I like this."

He gave an approving nod. "They get together every week or so and just play—random people each time. There are worse ways to pass time."

They listened to several songs, barely talking. When the band stopped for a break, Ian took a long look at Charlotte. "What are you thinking?"

"That I love this. It's so..." Suddenly at a loss for words, she grinned and shook her head.

"It's so... time for another drink. Is that what you meant?"

She leaned forward conspiratorially. "It's like you can read my mind."

He tossed her that grin that made her light up every time. "I'm sure I'd enjoy that even more than the music."

Before he could slide out of the booth, Charlotte put her hand on his wrist to stop him. "I've got this."

He frowned with mock disapproval. "Not this time. Maybe later." He leveled a penetrating gaze that nearly took her breath away, then he left for the bar before she could protest.

"Wow," she whispered. Her cheeks felt hot. She touched her face. *It's the wine. And the room. It's so hot.*

So was he.

IAN PULLED the Rover to a stop in the front of the castle. "Wait there." He walked around to her side, opened the car door, and offered his upturned palm for support. Charlotte took it, wishing she hadn't worn gloves. Once inside, Ian walked with her up the stairs. When they reached her room, Charlotte lifted her eyes to meet his. He was quiet and still. Without thinking, she found herself leaning closer, then she realized he was too. Her lips parted.

"We agreed to pretend to be friends," he said softly.

She lowered her eyes. "Yes, we did." What was she doing? Or rather, what was her heart doing—besides pounding? She glanced down the hall, anywhere but at him.

Her face must have revealed too much because he seemed compelled to explain. "There's something you should know about me. When I give my word, I keep it." The corner of his mouth turned up into a faint smile that brought a wistful light to his eyes. He shifted slightly away then turned back. "But I made no such promise of pretend friendship for tomorrow. What are your views on breakfast?"

"I'm a fan." Her heart swelled. This was way too happy to feel about breakfast.

"Would you mind if I joined you?"

"No." She answered a little too quickly, but if he noticed, he didn't look too disturbed.

"What time? I know you're not a morning person."

She grinned. "You're not either."

"I'd make an exception for you."

"I'm honored."

"As you should be," he said with a hint of a smirk.

Charlotte realized she was grinning, but she couldn't help herself. "How's nine o'clock?"

"Perfect. See you then."

"Good night, pretend friend." Charlotte opened her door and turned back to smile.

Ian touched her doorjamb and left.

FIVE

Two minutes early, Ian swooped into the chair opposite hers. "So, what's on the agenda today?"

She looked up from the menu, still startled. "I don't know. I haven't really decided. This is so unlike me. I usually have everything planned in advance, but..." She stopped herself. "There were some last-minute changes to the itinerary."

"Ah, yes. The boyfriend."

"Ex-boyfriend."

He leaned closer with a satisfied smile. "Even better."

She felt herself blush. "Anyway, my schedule's open."

He frowned and sucked in a breath through his teeth. "Oh, I should warn you—"

Before he could finish the thought, a server

appeared and filled his coffee. He smiled and thanked her, and the woman practically floated away—but not before casting a scrutinizing glance at Charlotte.

With an embarrassed smile, he said, "Sorry. They're not used to seeing me here. Well, that's not entirely true. They're not used to seeing me here with a lovely lady."

At that moment, Charlotte discovered she was not immune to flattery. It had been some time since she'd had the chance to put it to the test. When that realization had settled, a revelation struck her. She'd missed Ian's main point. The staff wasn't used to seeing the laird with random female guests. She couldn't help but be pleased about that. It settled one of the doubts that had cost her some sleep. She was not just another in a chain of guests who'd succumbed to his considerable charms—not that he needed all that much charm. His strong features and broad shoulders did half the job. And he was, after all, a laird. The fact that she hadn't fallen into a dead faint by then was a testament to her character—and maybe her balance.

She glanced up and caught his eyes fixed on her... again. She was rescued from making a stammering fool of herself by the arrival of their breakfast. As they proceeded to eat in comfortable silence, she wondered why this full Scottish breakfast idea hadn't caught on in the States.

Charlotte set her fork down and reached for her coffee. "Oh, weren't you going to warn me about something?"

"Yes, thank you. I was." He studied her thoughtfully. "About our pretending to be friends..." He looked up and sighed then gazed into her eyes. "The thing is, I couldn't have lasted much longer."

Because he can't stand me? She didn't want to jump to conclusions.

He leaned back and glanced about as though making sure he wouldn't be overheard. He leaned closer and spoke in a secretive tone. "Before we make plans for today, I feel it only fair to warn you." He peered into her eyes. "At some point today, I'm going to want to kiss you."

Charlotte was stunned into silence. It took all her resolve to avert her eyes from his lips. Doubt came over his face. She hadn't meant to make him feel that way. He'd just caught her off guard. She couldn't leave him wondering, but opening up didn't come easily to her. She met his unwavering gaze. "If that time comes, I'll manage to cope." An unabashed smile bloomed on her face. Where it came from, she couldn't begin to know. She felt as though she'd been set free.

Looking thoroughly pleased, Ian tilted his head toward the door. "Shall we?"

Charlotte rose and walked past his outstretched

arm. He followed, going by the wide-open eyes of the staff. Not only did they appear unaccustomed to seeing him with a woman, they seemed downright stupefied. That pleased her more than it should have, but she couldn't help herself. If years of being taken for granted had left her susceptible to even the slightest bit of encouragement, she was okay with it. She was going to enjoy her one glimpse of the sun as it broke through the clouds.

As THEY DROVE north along the coast, the sky grew unnaturally dark as a north wind blew dark clouds from the sea. Snow came in light flakes and flew at the windshield. Ian made an unscheduled U-turn and pulled over to the side of the road. "The storm was forecast for later, but here we are. I'm afraid the tour's off."

"That's okay."

He grimaced. "Not quite the dazzling day I was hoping for."

Charlotte shrugged. "Who said I'm not dazzled?" She'd meant it as a joke, but there was more truth in it than she cared to admit.

Ian's smile faded. He gave her hand a quick squeeze. "Let's get you safely home. Then we'll continue our tour inside Craigthorn." He put the car in gear and pulled onto the road.

Minutes later, he dropped Charlotte at the front entrance, and she waited for him to park the car in the garage. The doorman took her coat, then a waiter appeared from a doorway down the hall and offered her a small glass from a tray.

"What's this?"

"Drambuie."

"What is it?"

"Och, well, legend has it that it was Bonnie Prince Charlie's own recipe. No one knows exactly, but it's made up of Scotch whisky, honey, and an assortment of herbs and spices."

Charlotte took a sip. "Oh, it's good!"

The waiter retreated as Ian arrived from another door down the long hall, carrying a glass of his own. "Let's warm up by the fire." He led her to a sitting room, where they sat on a settee facing the fire. "I'm sorry to drag you out into the cold for no reason."

"I enjoyed the fresh air." His doubtful reaction made her smile. "I did," she insisted.

"As soon as you've warmed up, our tour will begin." He set his drink down and held out his hand, palm up. "Let's see."

She set down her drink and put her hand in his.

"Good God! It's frozen!" He rubbed it between his

hands then did the same with the other. "Slightly better. Come here." He led her to the fire. "Hold your hands out." He joined her in warming his hands.

After a minute or two, she looked up. "I think I'm okay now."

"Are you? Let's see." He put her hand to his cheek and held it there for a moment too long.

"Better?" Charlotte asked.

He turned and pressed his lips to her hand then softly said, "Aye." He lifted his eyes to meet hers, and her heart leaped.

Ian's eyes brightened. "So! Time for the tour. Come with me." He took her hand and led her up the stairs to a door that marked the end of the public portion of the castle. He let go of her hand while he entered a code in the keypad. She missed his touch. "I should warn you, it's not as shiny and polished as the public area, but there are some rooms here that I love." Not far down the hall, Ian held open a door. "Welcome to the gallery."

Charlotte walked into a large, rectangular room lined with portraits that hung against damask wall coverings. Faint ribbons of light shone through tall, narrow windows.

He switched on the lights. "Meet my family."

"Wow. Most people only get to meet two or three generations."

He grinned. "There's a bit more than that staring down at you now."

She laughed and looked at him. "If their eyes start to follow me, I'm out of here."

"Understood."

They went from one portrait to the next while Ian explained who the people were. Charlotte couldn't imagine having such a presence of family, their portraits, their possessions, dating back generations. "And they're all your ancestors."

He nodded.

She paused to study a portrait of a young Elizabethan woman.

Ian looked up at the painting. "Her name was Elinor. She was sixteen years old when this portrait was painted."

"She was beautiful but a little 'ruff' around the edges." Charlotte winced. "Because that collar is called a ruff. Sorry."

Ian made a face.

"I know. I wouldn't blame you at all for sending me to the dungeon." Her eyes widened. "Oh my gosh. You've probably got one."

"It's not part of the tour. Although if your jokes get any worse, I might reconsider."

"I wish I could say I can do better." She looked back at the portrait. "She looks very happy."

"Ah, well, that was probably the last time she did. Legend has it that she fell in love with a handsome young castle guard. When her father found out, he locked her in her room and sent her lover off to Europe to fight."

"Why?"

"He was beneath her in station. They would never have married."

It occurred to Charlotte that if they had lived back then, she wouldn't have been standing there with Ian. She probably would have had some sort of domestic position—with her luck, chamber pot duty.

Ian went on with the story. "Months turned into years. Although no longer confined to it, she took to her room and grew more despondent with each passing day. After five years, a messenger arrived from abroad and reported that the lover was dead, killed in battle."

"How sad."

"Aye. She was so devastated that she went down to the river and hanged herself from a tree limb."

"Oh my gosh, that's so tragic."

"And then the lad came home. They say Elinor can be seen sometimes walking the banks of the river."

"What happened to him?"

"I don't know. My ancestors only kept track of their own."

She looked about. "It's all so much larger than life —and it's your life. It's your normal."

"It is. But sometimes it gets a bit heavy to bear."

"But why? You've got all this amazing tradition around you! I mean look! It's a grand room filled with your family portraits—actual oil paintings—some from hundreds of years ago."

His mouth turned up at the corner as he lowered his eyes.

"I've got a few family photo albums and shoe boxes of loose photos. The rest is on social media sites. So you'll have to excuse me if I have a difficult time getting my head wrapped around this."

He looked charmingly bashful. "I assure you, it's not nearly as glamorous as you're making it sound. And I didn't bring you here to impress you. I brought you here to show you this." He took her hand and led her to a window seat in the far corner of the room. "This was my favorite place as a child." He gestured for her to sit down. "Please."

Charlotte sat and took in a thrilling view of the sea and the foaming waves flinging themselves against the rocks. "Oh, wow." Her eyes widened as she took it all in.

"This was the best place to read or to play with an old set of tin soldiers. I could be found here on rainy days, or snowy ones like today, or days when I wanted to get away."

"From what?"

"My parents. When they argued."

"Was that often?"

"Probably. But after I was sent off to school, I didn't hear them again."

She expected some sort of show of emotion, but his expression showed none. "How old were you?"

"When I went to boarding school? Eleven."

He said it so matter-of-factly that it made Charlotte wonder if he truly viewed it that way. Going away at that age would have shaken her sense of the world around her. Everything she had counted on would have shifted. "That must have been hard."

He shrugged it off. "You grow up, go to school. It's all part of life, isn't it?"

"Not my life."

Barely reacting, Ian turned toward the window. "Anyway, none of it mattered when I was here."

Charlotte hugged her knees to her chest. "I can see why. I could sit here and read all day long—or just stare at the sea."

"Both of which I've done many times." He exhaled. "Well. Shall we get on with the tour?"

Charlotte pulled herself out of the chair and walked over to one of the portraits.

"My grandfather," Ian said.

"I can see the family resemblance." She slowly followed Ian to the door. "Shouldn't you be up here somewhere?"

Ian shook his head. "I haven't felt the need. Although come here." He put his arm around her shoulders and pulled out his phone. "Smile, lass." He took a selfie of the two of them then propped his phone up on the chair-rail border. "There. Don't you look pretty? But who is that sorry muppet standing beside you?"

Charlotte fixed her eyes on the photo. "I don't think he's sorry at all."

"Or a muppet?" he asked with a mischievous light in his eyes.

"No, I don't think he's that either." She studied the selfie as if she were in a museum.

"Are you sure?" Ian asked. "Take your time. Give it some thought."

"No need." She picked up the phone and handed it to him. "I know what I like."

He nodded approvingly. "Ah, a woman of discriminating taste."

"Of course, I also love the velvet painting of dogs playing poker."

"Did I say discriminating? I meant disturbing."

"I'm not one to follow the crowd." She turned and

cheerfully walked to a window. "Oh, look at the snow."

He joined her at the window and clasped her hand. "Let's go get some books from the library and escape to the laird's room."

Charlotte's face lit up. "Excellent plan!"

They left, still holding hands.

AFTER A BRIEF STOP at the library, they arrived at another door much like the others. Ian entered the code.

"You're very high tech around here," Charlotte said.

"What, because of these?" He leveled a look. "Well, the truth is, I kept losing my keys. A laird shouldn't have to hunt down the housekeeper to get into his rooms. It's unseemly. Embarrassing, actually. So I made a few changes." He opened the door. "And here we have the laird's room."

Charlotte walked into the room, which had a small dining table and a sitting area near the fireplace at the end.

"There's a manager to handle the hotel-guest side of things. I try to stay behind the scenes as much as possible. I'm not one for idle chatter, so I tend to hide out here. I know. Not very hospitable of me, but there you have it. I'm a bit of a recluse."

"Hard to hide from the world when you live in a castle."

"Not as hard as you'd think, not with this many rooms."

"And each door with a keypad."

He nodded.

Charlotte sank into a chair. "I can't imagine being away at school as a child. You must have longed for home, or even a moment alone."

His sharp look softened. "Don't read too much into it. I'm really quite shallow."

Charlotte laughed. "Right."

Ian sat in the chair beside hers. "We can sit by the fire and read, or we could watch football on the big-screen telly."

"I don't recall seeing a tele—TV."

"It's hidden behind one of the paintings."

"Oh, I want something like that in my house. Or maybe I'll just do a budget version and hot-glue crown molding to the edge of my TV and play screensavers of paintings."

Ian looked unsure of how to react.

"I'm joking."

He exhaled. "Oh, thank God. I wasn't sure."

"After all the many... hours we've known one another, you still can't tell when I'm kidding?"

"I know. I'm horribly unobservant. I can't imagine why you even bother with me."

She lifted her eyes to meet his unwavering gaze. "I can." Charlotte didn't know how he managed to make it feel as if they'd always been together and always would be—timeless. *Whoa, slow down, Charlotte!* She forced a flippant smile. "I'm in it for the castle."

His demeanor changed in an instant. He frowned and stared at the door. "I've completely forgotten. I'm afraid I've got something to attend to. Come, I'll walk you back to your room."

Her jaw dropped. "What? But—okay." She hurried to catch up with him as he locked the door and strode down the hallway.

SIX

Charlotte forced herself to stop brooding. Ian had made himself scarce for the rest of the morning, and she had spent too much time trying to understand why. She finally heaved a sigh and went out for some fresh air. At the end of a vigorous two-mile walk, she arrived at the village square. There she sat at the foot of the mercat cross and took a drink from her water bottle. Spying a cafe nearby, she walked along the narrow sidewalk beside the main road and went inside. She was greeted with a warm "Hiya!" from a young woman Charlotte assumed was the owner.

Delicious aromas enveloped her. In the glass counter display was a tempting assortment of pastries and sweets. Charlotte must have missed the lunch rush. Only two tables were occupied. She chose a small table by the window and studied the menu. After settling on a bowl of homemade soup and a sandwich, she gave her order and turned her gaze to the wintery scene through the window.

The village was tranquil, with a few small shops and an occasional car driving by. From time to time, people passed the shop window. On down the road, at the edge of the village, was the pub Ian had taken her to. If it weren't for that, she might have added it to her mental list of places to go.

Garrett's original plan had been to venture out and perhaps hire a driver to show them around. But those were his plans with his budget. Charlotte didn't have the nerve to try driving, so there she was in the middle of nowhere—a gorgeous nowhere—but it was starkly remote. Still, she hadn't felt lonely until Ian had abruptly dropped her off at her room.

She sat in the café and wrote in her trip journal then gazed down the road and considered. She speculated as to whether Ian might be in the pub. He was the one who'd said he was a recluse. He was probably in the laird's room, hiding from her. He must have wanted some space, and she was quite willing to give it to him. If he thought she was a needy waif desperately clinging to him, then he didn't know her at all. The last thing she'd wanted when she came to the Highlands was a man in her life. In fact, she'd come for an escape from the last one. She'd come hoping to enjoy being alone and in charge of her days and her life.

How had she let Ian ruin it all? No, that wasn't fair. It was easy to blame someone else, but she had let it happen. She'd nearly lost herself once again. That seemed to be her pattern, which was all the more reason that being alone was the cure. Now that she saw how things were, she would be able to keep her attraction to Ian in check. "How hard can it be?" She was only there for a few more days.

That thought sank in. In a few days, she would be home, back at work, pulling sticky lollipops and gum from the pages of library books. She didn't have time to waste fretting over some man. She was in the Highlands of Scotland, staying in a castle, no less! She really didn't have cause to complain.

She paid the bill and headed out into the world— one she was resolved to enjoy.

CHARLOTTE SIGHED and set down the book she'd been trying to read. She had been back for an hour from her walk to the village. She'd taken a shower, stared out at the sea, tried to read, and was giving up. There was only so much time a person could spend all alone, and she'd hit her own personal wall. She had grown tired of reading, so the library was out. She was in an uncharacteristically talkative mood. Apparently, hours of silence did that to a person. So what better place to find conversation than a pub? There was a small pub in the castle that she hadn't visited yet. She wasn't keen on the idea of running into Ian, but he had his own stash of liquor, so the chance of him showing up there had to be slim. She felt like talking to someone—other than Ian—so she decided to risk it. If no one else cared to talk, there was always the bartender. It was his or her job to listen, poor thing.

Charlotte walked through the door and found the pub rich with historic character. The walls were clad in tartan wallpaper and dark oak moldings. In the late afternoon, dusk was already settling. Little light shone through the windows, leaving the bulk of the lighting job to the fire, a few wall sconces, and twinkle lights strung around the oak beams. In contrast to the rest of the castle, the room had a rough, old-world atmosphere, as though pirates and farmhands might appear side by side at the bar. She took a seat there and asked the bartender to recommend a scotch. She was more of a wine drinker, but when in Rome...

He poured her some samples, and she chose one that tasted a little of peat.

"Not everyone likes tasting the peat."

"I like it. It's earthy."

"Aye, that it is."

They were talking about New York when the door opened and let in the sound of male laughter followed by silence. In walked a man who appeared to be about Charlotte's age, late twenties, not quite Ian's height, dressed in tastefully casual clothing. He was followed by Ian. Charlotte inwardly groaned. Ian's companion glanced back and started to say something but stopped and studied Ian's expression. Ian held Charlotte's gaze. His friend followed Ian's gaze to Charlotte, and the questioning look on his face disappeared.

The room was too small to avoid an encounter. No doubt forced by proximity and impossibly good manners, Ian approached. "Charlotte Glass, I'd like you to meet Lewis Pritchard." As she shook hands with the man, Ian said, "Lewis and I are old friends."

"From school," Lewis added.

"Nice to meet you."

"Is that an American accent I detect?"

"Yes." She smiled cordially and waited a moment. "Well, if you'll excuse me, I've got to..." Her mind went blank. Go to an appointment? Feed the meter? She couldn't think of a thing. "Go. It was so nice to meet you, Lewis."

Lewis Pritchard was grinning, which didn't help her feel any less awkward.

She forced a quick glance at Ian. "Goodbye." Face

flushed, she walked out of the pub, rushed past some guests, and went straight to her room.

Once safely inside, she did a face-plant on the bed. She pounded her fist on the mattress then stood up and paced. "I can't stay here. I can't just dissolve into a stupid mess every time I run into him. But I can't afford to change my flight. I could see if there's a bus to Inverness. A hotel would be too much, but I might find an affordable hostel." She nodded and began to search on her phone. It wasn't as easy as she'd hoped it would be. But she grabbed the small notepad by the phone and began making lists.

An hour later, she leaned her head back against the chair and sighed. It wasn't going to work. There were too many moving parts and not enough money to make it all happen. She pulled a throw blanket over her lap and hugged her knees to her chest. The wind whistled outside, but in her room, it was cozy and warm. It was safe—except for her heart. She didn't know how this had happened, but she was not going to let it defeat her. She dialed down to the front desk and asked if she could have dinner brought to her room. Then she willed herself to block out the world. She would spend a comfortable evening in there. She had a book she could lose herself in. What more could she want?

"I'M A NUMPTY." Ian raked his fingers through his hair and looked across the pub's corner table.

Lewis shrugged. "I knew that."

"I was just being nice. She was here all alone. So I thought what harm could it do to show her around?"

Lewis lifted his eyebrow. "You, sir, are very good at your job. It's not enough that you open your home to perfect strangers, but you are truly the quintessential host. I've never seen anything like it." He leaned back with a satisfied gleam in his eyes. "Your guest... Charlene?"

Ian glared. "Charlotte." Lewis knew very well what her name was.

"Charlotte, that's right. She's quite pretty."

He eyed Lewis through narrow eyes. "Oh, really?" Anyone could see that. What Lewis didn't know was how clever she was and how she made him laugh. Nothing else seemed to matter when he was with her.

Lewis cleared his throat.

Ian looked at him. Could this man do nothing but grin? It was so damned annoying.

Lewis took a sip from his glass. "Since you were just being nice, I thought you wouldn't mind if I asked her to join me for dinner."

"Oh, you did? Well, we're booked," Ian practically barked.

"Oh. Well, I'll take her out somewhere else, then."

"No, you won't."

Lewis's overdone show of surprise couldn't fool anyone, least of all Ian. "But I thought... Oh. You... and she? That's odd. I was sure I saw icicles forming on her shoulders. Must be the weather."

"Yeah, well, it's my fault. I hit the brakes pretty hard. I deserved what I got."

For the first time, Lewis looked serious. "You like her."

Ian stared off toward the door then glowered at his whisky. "I can't like her." He lowered his voice. "And you know why."

Lewis shook his head. "She's not at all like Phoebe."

"And how do you know?"

"Because nobody else could be Phoebe Forsythe, and that's a good thing."

Ian rolled his eyes. "I don't think she's at all like her, but then I didn't think Phoebe was like that, either."

"What, after your money?"

Ian laughed. "Yeah, my money."

"So, problem solved. If she's not after your money, then what's the problem?"

"Other than her leaving in a few days and putting an ocean between us? It's a match made in heaven."

"You're right. Love should only happen between people who live in the same place."

"Wait! No one said anything about love."

Lewis wrinkled his face. "No?"

"No!" Ian added emphatically. He avoided looking at Lewis as long as he could.

"You don't have to say it to feel it."

Ian tried to protest. "I've just known her for a few days."

Lewis looked at his watch. "Well, at this rate, I expect an engagement by, oh, teatime tomorrow?"

"Very funny."

"Actually, it's quite sad from where I'm sitting." Lewis got up and went to the bar for another round.

Ian exhaled. Lewis was right. He had feelings for Charlotte. He wouldn't call it love. But the feelings were there, and the whole thing was hopeless. Which was why he had cut it off so abruptly. She'd unwittingly brought it on herself when she'd said she was in it for the castle. Of course, she hadn't meant it, but it had touched a raw nerve left over from Phoebe.

Lewis set down their drinks and sank into his chair. "Talk to her."

"There's no future there."

"Maybe not. Either way, do you not think that knowing is better than wondering?"

"I don't know."

"Neither does she. Talk to her."

Ian frowned and stared at his glass. Maybe he should.

Lewis leaned forward. "Right now, she's probably up there in her room, wondering why you've been acting like such a numpty." His eyes sparkled. "This way, she'll know it's because you *are* one."

Ian reached over to swat him with the back of his hand, but Lewis leaned back out of his reach and laughed. "Just talk to her, eejit."

SEVEN

Charlotte peered into the video-chat window on her phone. "He runs hot and cold, worse than the castle faucets."

Her friend Jen leaned closer to the camera. "What did you say to him?"

Charlotte threw her hands up. "I don't know! I wish I had a transcript. I think I said something about how I was in it for the castle."

Jen seemed as confused as Charlotte. "In what?"

"In this... well, I can't call it a relationship. Hanging out with him. I mean, I just said it. It wasn't a big deal."

"To you."

Charlotte frowned. "Well, yeah. Obviously."

"In it for the castle?" Jen looked up, thinking. "But that *is* why you're there."

"I know. Oh! Shh!"

"I didn't say anything!"

"Jen, I gotta go. Someone just slipped something under the door."

"Your bill already?"

"No. I don't know. I'll text you later." Charlotte waved and set down her phone. She walked over to the door and picked up the envelope. It was on Craigthorn stationery, so it did actually look like a bill. *But this early?* Maybe Ian was kicking her out. She opened it.

"Please meet me in the library. I've been an eejit."

He hadn't even signed it. Maybe he was afraid a maid might come across it. But Charlotte knew who it was from, as he knew she would. There was no meeting time on the note. No explanation.

She exhaled. Was she supposed to drop everything and go running to the library just because he'd asked her to? *No! Absolutely not!* She would walk. Slowly. After putting on makeup and brushing her hair. Well, the least she could do was look good while she looked angry.

When she was ready to go, Charlotte stopped in her tracks and stared into the mirror. "Goal setting, Charlotte: you will not—repeat, not—allow him or anyone else to treat you like Garrett did, castle or not." With that, she took a deep, cleansing breath and walked out of her room.

CHARLOTTE PAUSED OUTSIDE THE LIBRARY. Voices, some unfamiliar, including Ian's, were coming from the other side of the door. She hesitated then walked in. Ian sat opposite his favorite chair, facing the door. He was talking with an American couple who sounded as though they were from Texas or maybe Oklahoma. The husband was broad-shouldered with a middle-aged paunch, and the wife was slender and well-dressed with an impressive layer of makeup and hairspray. Charlotte hesitated inside the doorway, but Ian beckoned her to join them.

The couple was in the midst of discussing the places they'd visited so far on their trip—in some detail, as it turned out—when Ian politely interrupted them to introduce Charlotte.

Before he could even begin, the man extended his hand. "Jack Jackson." They shook hands. "And this is my better half, Adaline."

"Nice to meet you," Charlotte said.

The conversation picked up where they'd left off. Ian was an impeccable host, attentive and gracious, as the laird of a castle should be. And Charlotte could not fault the couple. They finished describing their travels and focused on Ian, clearly fascinated with him. So was Charlotte but for entirely different reasons.

Ordinarily, she wouldn't have minded passing the time with a pleasant chat with some fellow travelers, but at the moment, she could barely feign interest. From the direct glances she was catching from Ian, they were on the same page.

Charlotte glanced at her watch. "Well, I'm off." She stood and said her goodbyes then turned toward the door. After a pause, she turned back to Ian. "I'm a bit turned around. How do I get to the front door from here?"

"It's right down the hall there," Jack Jackson said. "You'll see the stairs. You can't miss it."

Charlotte feigned confusion. "Oh, I wouldn't count on that."

Jackson's forehead creased as he studied Charlotte. He wasn't buying her bewilderment. Apparently, his thirty years in the used-car business had taught him to read people well.

"I'll show you." Ian flashed his winning grin, gave a hasty farewell, and whisked Charlotte out of the room.

Jackson said, "But you can see it right there from the door. If it were a snake it would've bit you." He started to get up, but Adaline pulled him down by the elbow.

Adaline said, "Honey, what is the matter with you? Can't you see...?"

As Ian and Charlotte walked briskly down the

corridor, Charlotte said, "I'm impressed."

"With the Jacksons?"

"No, by our escape. I'm forever getting trapped talking with people at parties after everyone else slips away. It's a curse."

"Is it? Being nice?" The light in his eyes seemed to have nothing to do with the topic at hand.

His show of warmth was too much of a contrast with his earlier behavior. They'd both overlooked it while in the presence of others, but he'd put an invisible but palpable wall between them that would not be easily breached.

Ian took her hand. "Sorry about having to meet like that, but I didn't want to go to your room. For one thing, the staff would have noticed. So I thought the library was the best. We're on our way to the laird's room."

"Didn't you think I'd be able to find it?"

"I didn't want to risk your having trouble with the digital lock."

"I can punch in a series of numbers."

"I know. But I didn't want to take any chances."

She gave him a questioning frown.

"Yes, I'm an eejit, especially where you're concerned." They went into the laird's room and sat near the fire. "Charlotte, I'm sorry. Earlier, what happened—it wasn't your fault."

Charlotte was even more confused. Ian was behaving strangely enough as it was—well, strangely for him. Since she'd known him, which, granted, wasn't that long, he had always been poised and said the right words. But this bright and socially adept man was now glancing about, tapping his fingers on his knee, and looking downright nervous.

He leaned closer. "We've shared battle scars, but I didn't tell you all of mine. My girlfriend became my ex-girlfriend when I learned that she was in love with the idea of life in a castle and all it entailed. I just happened to come along with the bargain. To be honest, I didn't take it well. It was a bit of a blow to the ego. So when you said you were in it for the castle, it touched a raw nerve."

"I can see how it would. But you know I was joking."

"I did, and yet I couldn't help but wonder if there was some truth in the joke."

"I'm not like that," Charlotte said softly.

"I should have explained myself to you."

Charlotte nodded. "It must be a guy thing—not wanting to talk about feelings."

"I wish it were only that, but it's a bit more extreme for me."

"How so?"

He didn't answer at first. "It's taken a few years of

therapy to get even this far—talking with you. I'm told I'm a bit buttoned up."

Charlotte wouldn't have described him like that. But then, how many people would describe her as shy?

"I told you I went to boarding school. Let's just say it was a challenge. I learned to cope by keeping my cards pretty close to the vest, but when my parents died while I was away, that more or less finished me off."

"I'm so sorry." Charlotte didn't know what else to say. Opening up to her couldn't be easy for him, and he was practically spilling his guts.

Ian exhaled and ran his fingers through his hair. "Well, I suppose the main point is I have trust issues."

"That's understandable. At a young age, you had everything that you counted on taken away."

"Aye." His eyes lingered on the fire, then he turned toward her. "You're probably wondering why I would tell you all this." His gray eyes were open and honest. "I didn't want you to leave here believing you'd done something wrong. And I suppose I didn't want you to think I was angry." He shifted his weight on the settee then rubbed his forehead. "No, that's not it, either. Damn." He let out a frustrated sigh. "This is completely ridiculous. We've only just met. You'll be going home soon. And here I am rambling like... like some sort of..."

Charlotte's heart ached seeing him struggle. The poor guy was clearly distraught, and she wasn't much better.

He took her hands in his. "Charlotte, what I'm trying to say is I... like you."

"I like you too." She looked into his eyes, but he shut his eyes and lowered his head, almost wincing.

"I suppose that's enough for now. Or ever." He lifted his eyes to meet hers. "I'm sorry. I didn't mean to hurt you. And I'd hate for you to leave thinking I'm some sort of... a..."

"Jerk?" Charlotte's lips spread into a warm smile.

"Well, I'll take that since it's better than what I was thinking." His eyes twinkled as he offered his usual endearing smile.

"That's not at all what I think."

He'd regained his composure, but Charlotte knew she'd just been given a rare glimpse beyond his appealing façade. A sudden urge struck her. She leaned over and kissed him. She told herself that an innocent gesture wouldn't do any harm. It was only a kiss, a light touch of the lips, a simple show of affection. It was harmless. He'd just told her he liked her. And she liked him too. It couldn't go anywhere. She would only be there for the rest of the week. But the feelings were real.

She could still feel the touch of his lips as she

leaned away. It was only a kiss. It was practically chaste.

But then Ian took her face in his hands and kissed her—really kissed her. She forgot how to breathe.

Charlotte pulled away just before launching herself onto his lap and returning the favor. But oh, how she wanted to do just that. The worst thing she could do was follow her heart. That hadn't gone well in the past. She had her own issues, and a relationship with Ian wouldn't help.

But she still let him kiss her again. More than that, she kissed him back. Her heart opened up to a rush of emotion. He had to have felt it as strongly as she did. They'd wandered into exposed and vulnerable places —places where love happened. Places where pain happened too. It was only a matter of time.

Ian found the wherewithal to stop and hold her at arm's length. "Too fast?"

She couldn't even manage to nod, but he seemed to understand her anguished sigh.

His eyes ached with longing, but he shook his head and forced a smile as he got up and pulled her to her feet. "In lieu of a cold shower, I've got the next best thing. Come with me." He grabbed a throw blanket and led her by the hand to the door.

"Okay?" She wondered about the blanket. She didn't know about his bed, but hers came supplied. So where else could they have been going? Obviously, someplace cold. One thing was certain—the man wasn't boring.

Ian led Charlotte up a series of narrow stone stairs. "I used to play here and imagine the sword fights that took place long ago."

"It's so narrow. How did they even manage?"

Ian paused to look at her. "With great difficulty."

Charlotte smirked and climbed the rest of the stairs. At the top stood a thick wooden door, which Ian opened. He took hold of Charlotte's hand and led her out onto the battlements. "Watch your step. It's uneven. We can't have you falling."

"Too late for that," she muttered.

"Sorry?"

"Oh, nothing."

Ian paused and wrapped the blanket around both their shoulders. Charlotte leaned close and looked out at the snow-dusted fields and hills lit by moonlight.

"I like to come here to think when something's on my mind," Ian said.

"And is something on your mind now?"

Without turning to face her, he said, "Yes."

Charlotte studied his face. She couldn't read it. "Am I supposed to guess?"

He tossed her a quick glance. "I'd rather you didn't."

Clouds drifted in front of the moon, leaving them in near darkness except for a light over the doorway. Her irrational childhood fear of the dark threatened to seize her, so she stayed close to Ian.

"You."

She peered at him. "Excuse me?"

"You're on my mind—have been since I met you."

Charlotte couldn't speak.

"Please tell me you're smiling," Ian said. "If you aren't—if you're shocked or revolted—please lie."

"No."

"You're not smiling? I see. Before you say anything else, would you give me a moment to brace myself?"

"No, I'm not revolted."

"Oh, thank God."

She was heartened to hear the relief in his voice and to feel his arm about her shoulders.

"Charlotte, I don't know what this is. If you lived here or I lived there, we'd have time to find out."

She exhaled.

"This was a terrible idea," Ian said.

"No, I'm glad that we're talking."

"Not that. Coming up here at night. I thought it

would be romantic, but I'm freezing my arse off, and I can't see your face. For all I know, you're about to burst into laughter."

"I assure you I'm not."

"I can hear it in your voice."

"Okay, now I'm smiling, but not in a bad way."

"Is there a good way when I'm the object of your amusement?"

"Yes." She couldn't help herself. All of her efforts at restraint might as well have been tossed over the edge of the battlements. The truth was, she was thrilled that Ian felt anything for her. The fact that he was undone over his feelings for her made her heart swell. She slipped her arms around his waist and buried her face in his chest. "It's okay."

"You're certainly taking all this in stride. Oh God, I've assumed that you felt the same way." He combed his fingers through his hair then put his hands on her arms and put distance between them. "This is madness. Let's go inside."

Charlotte was confused, but she was also cold. She would straighten things out someplace warm.

When she realized Ian was heading toward her room, Charlotte stopped. "No. We can't leave things like this."

"Like what?" Ian was back to his usual, controlled self, except Charlotte knew better.

"Unresolved."

He turned toward her with a look on his face that mirrored hers. She wasn't sure whether she felt more confused or frustrated.

"More talking?" He made a face as though talking were medicine. With a slight nod, he headed back toward the laird's room.

His first priority was to get a fire going in the fireplace. With that accomplished, he took Charlotte's hands and pulled her to her feet. Taking her face in his hands, he searched her eyes. "Tell me the truth. If it's bad, say it quickly."

She shook her head. *How can he even wonder?* But he took her movements as bad news and looked so disappointed.

"It's good," she hastened to say.

He lifted his eyebrows. "How good?"

Charlotte wanted to smile, not because it was funny to see this side of him, but because she'd been feeling just as nervous. She still couldn't believe what was happening. "I'm crazy about you!"

He exhaled. "Just once more."

"With feeling?"

At last, he relaxed and smiled.

"I am crazy about y—"

He kissed her. It came with a rush of pent-up passion that made Charlotte's head swim. Neither of them seemed ready to end it, but a knock on the door did the job.

Ian's eyes shone as he gazed at her. "Excuse me."

Ivy arrived with two cups of hot cocoa that Ian had ordered when they'd first arrived in the room. With all the excitement—and kissing—Charlotte had completely forgotten about it. Ivy was heading for the table to set down the tray, when Ian took it from her. "Thank you, Ivy. I'll take it from here."

She gave Ian a curious glance that revealed what she was too discreet to ask. With a quick nod to Charlotte, she left.

After Ivy was well on her way, Charlotte said, "I hope this won't make things awkward for you." He peered curiously at her, so she continued. "Having the staff know. About us. Not that there's an us necessarily, but—"

"I beg to differ." He walked swiftly to her, pulled her into his arms, and planted a kiss on her that made her knees nearly buckle. He released her just as she thought she might swoon and land in a melted blob on the floor. His eyebrow lifted ever so slightly. "There is an us. Necessarily."

"Point taken," she said breathlessly. She wondered if she would ever regain the use of her slack jaw. "But still, Ivy saw us here. In your room."

"It's more of a sitting room. I sleep in a different

room entirely, so scandal averted. But if you'd like, we could string up a rope across the middle of the settee while we talk."

"Very funny, but—"

He touched his forehead to hers. "I don't mind. And besides, they haven't had much to talk about lately. I owe it to them."

She frowned as she thought about the staff's reaction. *Why should I care?*

"Charlotte. Have some hot cocoa." He smiled and held out a cup.

Halfway through the cocoa, she put her cup down. "Ian, what day is it?"

He shrugged. "Wednesday." He looked at his watch. "Well, actually, no. It's officially Thursday."

Charlotte mentally counted the days and tried not to let it bother her.

"And you leave..."

"Sunday."

Their eyes met, then Charlotte stared at the fire and wondered. She was falling in love. *We only have three days together. Why am I doing this to myself?*

She thought for a moment.

Because I have to.

EIGHT

CHARLOTTE AWOKE on the laird's room settee with her feet on Ian's lap. He was sprawled on the other side of the settee with his feet on the old trunk that served as a table. The fire had died down to glowing embers, but they were kept warm by a couple of tartan throw blankets and each other. They'd stayed up talking into the night and had arrived at an understanding before falling asleep. They'd agreed that chemistry was a formidable force, one that had caused them to panic, each in their own way. But their feelings were strong, even if they couldn't quite reconcile them in the context of there being no feasible future for them. In the end, they decided to spend as much time together as they could. When the time came, they would part with good memories.

Once she calmed down and warmed up by the fire,

Ian did a remarkable job of describing how the rest of the week would be—so much so that Charlotte asked, "Will you draw up the papers? We'll need a witness. Maybe Ivy or Robby?"

He gave her a questioning look.

Charlotte burst into laughter. "I'm kidding!"

But they'd both, at least figuratively, signed off on the plan as if it weren't destined to fail.

When that was settled, they shared hopes and dreams, talked of their families, and divulged a few childhood stories. Peace settled between them like morning mist on the moors, because now they knew that perhaps the most powerful feelings a person could know were returned. Just before they surrendered to sleep, they formed a pact. Neither would mention their parting until the day came.

Not a word.

THEY WALKED out the front door, past the gauntlet of Ivy and Robby, who froze with awkward smiles on their faces when they caught sight of Ian and Charlotte. They recovered enough to greet Ian and Charlotte warmly and wish them a nice day.

As the door closed behind them, Charlotte looked

sideways at Ian. "You know they were talking about us, right?"

"Aye? Let them." He put his arm about her. "I hope they're watching us too." He stopped and swung Charlotte into his arms then dipped her backward and planted a deep, soulful kiss on her lips. Then he brought her back up to her feet and proceeded as though nothing had happened.

"Well, okay. Glad that's settled," Charlotte said with wide eyes.

As they walked, Ian reached over and clasped her hand. "Shall we walk or drive?"

"Walk. It's not too cold, and there's almost some sun behind all those gray clouds." They quietly walked for a while. "So... you went to boarding school, and then..."

"Uni."

"Which one?"

"St. Andrews." He smirked at her. "Why do I feel as though I ought to be at a table with a single lightbulb above my head?"

Charlotte shrugged matter-of-factly. "Because I'm interrogating you."

"Ah! So you admit it!"

"Yes. Because if I don't know everything about you, I can't make an informed decision."

He frowned. "About what?"

"About how much I like you. You've worked your way up the scale, by the way."

"Great. How many stars do I rate?"

"Five stars, at least!"

"Good. Because I only kiss girls who give me five stars."

Charlotte stopped and looked up expectantly. "Well, I've delivered my part of the bargain."

Ian tilted his head thoughtfully. "It's not really a bargain, is it? Look how I've had to work for those stars."

"Fair enough. So you're opting out?" She started to walk, but he swung her back into his arms.

"I didn't say that." To prove the point, he kissed her then looked around furtively. With no one to observe them, he led Charlotte to a tree and pinned her against it with the full length of his body.

"They're just stars," she whispered between kisses.

"To hell with the stars," he said and kissed her again.

Charlotte felt a bit wobbly kneed by the time they resumed walking, but a line came to mind. "Don't let's ask for the stars. We have the moon."

He laughed. "Other way around."

"I know. Wait! You have not seen that film!"

"Just some scenes. I took a film-studies class."

"You, sir, are full of surprises."

They walked along laughing and talking, both of which came effortlessly to them, as did silence. She didn't know all that much about Ian, but she didn't need to know every fact to know that they fit. Except for the part about living on separate continents. Charlotte stopped herself. *Girl, what are you doing? You're practically planning the wedding! Just stop. Just stop now.*

"What're you thinking about?"

It was scary how he could almost read her mind. She tried to look casual. "Why?"

"You were frowning."

She forced a pleasant smile. "Oh, I just thought about something from work." She shuddered. "Blech! I hope that doesn't happen again."

IAN AND CHARLOTTE left the café and went window-shopping along the high street. Some Christmas gift items in a shop window caught Charlotte's eye, and they went into the shop for a look.

A small bell rang as the door opened behind them.

"Ian, hello."

Charlotte and Ian both turned to find a smartly dressed woman—a very pretty woman—about their same age.

"Hello." He stared blankly at her, and she stared back at him.

Charlotte looked from one of them to the other and back again before deciding she couldn't take any more. She extended her hand to the woman. "Hi, I'm Charlotte Glass."

Ian recovered. "I'm sorry. This is—"

"Phoebe Forsythe." The woman had a knowing expression, as if her name should mean something to Charlotte.

"Nice to meet you." Charlotte tried to keep her expression neutral, despite a noticeable tension in the air.

The young woman repeated her name as she peered at Charlotte. "Phoebe. Forsythe?" She shot a sharp look at Ian. "You haven't told her?" Then she turned to Charlotte. "I'm the ex."

Charlotte was stunned but recovered after a second.

Phoebe smiled as she watched Charlotte's reaction.

Something about that self-satisfied smile rubbed Charlotte the wrong way. Or maybe she was just having a jealous reaction to meeting Ian's ex-girlfriend. Whatever it was, she felt small and petty, which wasn't like her.

"Well, don't let us keep you," Ian said. "We're all busy with last-minute shopping."

Phoebe stayed where she was like some potted plant. If plants smiled. Smugly. "Oh, I'm done with my shopping."

"Good for you. We're not. Charlotte?" He tilted his head toward the door then touched Charlotte's elbow.

They travelled a full block before he slowed down. "I am so sorry you had to endure that."

"Ian, I'm fine." She'd gone with her first instinct, to act as though nothing were wrong, but it was. The whole thing had been miserably awkward.

"It took me too long to realize that she's simply not a nice person. But you shouldn't have to suffer for my past mistakes."

"It's all right. If you're ever in New York, I'll be sure to introduce you to my ex-boyfriend for revenge."

He smiled gently.

Charlotte's eyes lit up. "Or maybe we could introduce them to each other." She'd been joking, but she thought for a moment. "Actually, they'd be perfect together."

Ian shook his head. "Enough about them. Let's talk about us."

"Okay. What about us?"

"How lucky we are that we're not with them."

She nudged her shoulder against his. "Way to change the subject, Ian."

IAN WAS quiet all through dinner, and after, he suggested they watch a movie together. Charlotte thought he was probably tired of talking. *And why wouldn't he be?* They'd been trying to squeeze weeks, if not months, of conversation into their short time together. That pace could not be sustained.

As they lay stretched out together on a love seat facing the television in Ian's suite of rooms, Ian turned off the closing credits and turned to Charlotte. "There's something I need to tell you."

Charlotte sat up a bit straighter. "That sounds ominous."

He dismissed her concern with a shake of his head but averted his eyes. "It shouldn't affect you. You'll be leaving, so—"

"Um, excuse me, but we had an agreement. No discussing the, uh, that which should not be discussed." Her effort to lighten the mood failed.

"Right. So I thought there was no point in bringing it up."

"Okay."

"Seeing Phoebe today..."

That killed Charlotte's good mood. She did not like the woman.

"I don't trust her," Ian said. "She's been rather

unkind about... things having to do with the breakup, and I'm afraid she might try to hurt you."

Charlotte was thoroughly confused. "How could Phoebe hurt me?"

He exhaled and looked up at the large wooden beams in the ceiling. "There's no easy way to say this, so I may as well forge ahead."

Charlotte watched him intently as he nervously shifted his position in his chair. "Oh my God. You're a vampire, aren't you?"

He flinched. "What? No!"

"I'm sorry. I just thought... You were being so ominous. I couldn't help myself."

He ran his fingers through his hair. "I told you I broke up with Phoebe when I learned she cared more for the castle. I just happened to come with it. I'm sure she would have preferred a title, as well, but she settled. Apparently, I was the best she could do, poor girl."

She smiled gently. "We have women like Phoebe in America."

Her remark barely registered with him. "Yes, well, before that, things got to a point where we were discussing a future."

Charlotte wasn't sure she wanted to hear it, but he seemed so upset that she thought he needed to have his say to feel better. She patiently waited.

"As you know, Craigthorn Castle has been in my family for hundreds of years. It has held up quite well. Unfortunately, the money hasn't."

Charlotte wanted to sigh with relief. "Is that all?"

He looked shocked. "*Is that all?*"

Charlotte leaned forward. "You're healthy. You haven't got some tragic addiction. Yes, I know that money issues can seem overwhelming, but you can get through this. And you will."

He leaned back in his chair. "Wow. This is the polar opposite of how Phoebe reacted."

She lifted her eyes with a guilty expression. "Is this the part where I should act surprised?"

At last, his mouth turned up at the corner, and the Ian she knew looked into her eyes. "You're..." He sighed. "I don't know. You're..."

"Am I?"

He grinned then shut his eyes and exhaled. A muscle in his cheek twitched. Only then did Charlotte realize he was choking back emotion.

"Ian," she whispered. "What did you think was going to happen when you told me?"

He smirked. "Well, Phoebe said I couldn't afford her, and she left."

"You can afford me." *But I'll have to leave too.* The thought saddened her.

He leaned over and kissed her. "I don't know how I can afford you. You are a rare and precious thing."

Charlotte's face lit up, but her heart was too full of emotion. She couldn't lose control yet, so she rolled her eyes. "Oh. So I'm a thing?"

"A rare and precious thing, yes."

His eyes were so full of adoration, the thought of losing him made her heart ache. She couldn't pretend anymore to take anything lightly. Instead, she gazed into his eyes, knowing that he would see what was in her heart. "Ian."

"I know."

NINE

As they talked over breakfast, Charlotte noticed Ivy and Robby with their heads together, smiling and stealing glances at Ian and Charlotte.

Ian caught Ivy looking their way. "Aye, they act like they've never seen a couple before."

"Maybe they just like seeing you happy—assuming you are."

She cast an unsure look at him that made Ian laugh as he put his hand on hers. "Aye, I am. Very happy."

Charlotte and Ian were getting good at long periods of gazing. She couldn't really blame Ivy or Robby for enjoying the show. She could only imagine how they must appear. But as they finished breakfast, Charlotte turned her thoughts to practical matters. "I think we should look at the books."

Ian wrinkled his face in surprise. "Have you studied accounting?"

"What?" She laughed. "No, not those kinds of books. The ones in your library."

"Okay?"

She nodded. "And maybe some paintings." When she saw his confusion, she added, "To sell."

"No." He was calm but resolved. In fact, he looked exactly how she imagined a laird should—strong and resolute.

"But Ian, it only makes sense."

"Do you think I haven't thought of that already? I could get a good price for the land—sell it off piece by piece."

"I'm not talking about selling your land. But you've probably got some rare books in that library of yours. Would a few books really make all that much of a difference?"

Ian's eyes shifted about, and he lowered his voice. "Scotland is full of castles. To you, this must look like just another of many. But this is my home, and it's all I have left of my family. I don't expect you to understand."

"Why not? Because my home's not a castle? I've got family."

His eyes narrowed. "And they're still alive."

His statement landed like a blow. She gave it some

thought. "You're right. I don't understand. But I do want to help. Why won't you let me?"

"Because it's not for you to help me!"

Charlotte closed her eyes and took a few calming breaths. When she felt she was ready, she spoke in quiet, even tones. "I'm not going to make a scene. I'm going to get up. And after I'm out of view from prying eyes, I'm going anyplace else that you're not." Without waiting for him to agree, she set down her napkin to the left of her plate, smiled at Ivy and Robby, then walked through the door.

"Charlotte," Ian called behind her.

She ignored him and left.

IAN EVENTUALLY FOUND her along one of the footpaths, on a bench overlooking the sea. He sat down beside her. "You're right. It makes sense to sell off what I can to make money. This isn't the first time the subject has come up."

He didn't know how to tell her how he felt without seeming weak. If he'd learned nothing else from boarding school, he'd learned that. They went after the weak ones. It had taken months, but he'd become one of the strong ones. With that accomplished, he'd remained quiet and observant. It was the only control he'd had.

He was a grown man now, but those feelings were hardwired. Craigthorn was his home. No matter what or who came and went from his life, he always had the castle as his fortress. Within the stone walls, with all of its rooms and its relics, he had something to stand on that was as solid as the rocks it was made of. He couldn't give it up—any of it. Charlotte had had no idea what she was asking.

She looked out at the sea. "I've upset you. It was not my intention. For a moment, I forgot that I'm not really part of your life."

"Why would you say that?" How could she not know she was part of his life? She was so much more than that. She was in his heart, and her absence would cause a gaping void there. Of course, he hadn't given voice to such thoughts. If he did, he would sound unbalanced. Yet he had every intention of giving their relationship time—time to grow, time for them to be certain. But he'd known almost at once that she was someone he could spend his life with. Once he said something like that, it could not be unsaid. Even so, she had to know how he felt. Still, waiting was the sensible thing.

"Ian." She leveled a practical gaze. "Today's Saturday."

"I thought we agreed not to mention it."

She ignored the reminder. "One of the things I love about you—"

Time stopped for a moment. She'd just used the L word, and he hadn't seemed to notice. But she had.

She continued. "Is your wholehearted enthusiasm. You get genuinely enthusiastic about things, and I love sharing that with you. So we both got a little ahead of ourselves. It was fun and exciting, and that was okay. It was more than okay; it was great. I have loved every minute of it."

There was that word again.

Charlotte looked straight at him. "But I crossed the line. You were right. It wasn't my place."

Ian leaned forward. "That is not what I said."

"Not in so many words."

He shook his head. "Charlotte." He opened his mouth to protest and explain himself, but she stood up.

"I'm sorry," she said.

"I'm not, because for almost a week, I've been happy, and I know that if things were different..." She looked into his eyes, and he stopped. He couldn't conjure the words. He felt every emotion he saw in her brown, watery eyes because he felt them too.

She suddenly smiled, and that tipped him over the edge. She was breaking his heart, or maybe they were breaking each other's hearts. What did it matter? The result was the same.

"Ian, you will be fine because you're amazing. Whatever happens, you'll figure it out." She kissed him on the forehead and whispered, "Without me."

Each footstep rang in his ears as she walked away.

CHARLOTTE HID in her room for the rest of the evening and packed with her phone propped up on a pillow and Jen's face on the messaging screen. "It's not like I'm mad or anything. It's just that it was a wake-up call, and I really didn't want to wake up. We'd been doing so well, living in the now with no thought for the future."

Jen folded her arms. "Deluding yourselves?"

"Yeah, pretty much." Charlotte paused with a folded shirt in her hand. "You know, delusions are highly underrated. I liked mine a lot."

Jen shook her head. "But that's not a sustainable option."

"I know." Charlotte slumped on the bed. "It was doomed from the start."

Jen offered a sympathetic look but no magic cure.

Charlotte barely noticed. "The thing is, I get what he was saying. There is absolutely no reason I should even have offered advice. It's not like I'd be here to live with the consequences. They're not mine to live with. I wish he was mine to live with." She shut her eyes. "He has such an incredible ass. Have I mentioned that?"

Jen grinned. "No. But I admire your ability to focus on the salient points."

"Well, somebody's got to." Charlotte picked up the phone. "Dang, I wish you were here!"

"What? And leave all these sticky children's books? You know that you're missing the only season in New York when you can't smell the urine."

"Oh, don't think I haven't thought about that! It's hell here—fresh air and a room in a castle overlooking the sea."

"Poor thing." Jen scowled. "So what are you going to do now?"

Charlotte sighed. "What I want to do is go pound on his door, fling myself into his arms—preferably after he opens the door—and hang on until he has to peel my clinging body from his."

"So you're going for subtlety."

Charlotte smirked. "Yeah."

"Seriously, honey, you've got to talk through this together. Even if it's goodbye. Do it right. Don't leave things hanging."

Charlotte squinted and moved the phone closer. "Did you really just say that?"

"Oh, crap. You know what I meant."

"Uh, yeah. Thanks for the advice—and the mental image." They both laughed, then Charlotte ended the call.

"Talk through this? No. I just can't."

ROOM SERVICE KNOCKED on the door. Charlotte got up from where she'd been staring at the fire to go get her dinner. She was perfectly happy hibernating in her room until it was time for her flight. Robby had even stopped and offered to drive her to the airport. It wasn't standard policy for guests, but he'd offered his services to her, anyway. She suspected that Ivy had put him up to it, or maybe Ian had arranged it out of guilt or a sense of obligation.

Charlotte opened the door. "Ian?"

He stood holding a room-service tray. "Don't blame Ivy or Robby. It's my fault."

"You paid them off to inform you of my room-service orders?"

He shrugged. "Well, sort of. They're already on the payroll."

Charlotte found him, as ever, irresistibly charming. At the same time, she loathed herself for succumbing to it. "Well, you'd better come in."

He came in and set down the tray as she shut the door behind him.

"I didn't order all that."

A bashful smile bloomed on his face. "I was hoping..."

"That I'd eat it all, and my resulting weight would ground the plane?"

He lifted an eyebrow. "Actually, no. But the idea has merit."

He gazed into her eyes until Charlotte could not escape it. She would never be able to stay angry with the man. "Ian, I'm sorry."

"For what?"

That was why she didn't go into business. She would have sucked at negotiating.

He stepped closer and brushed her cheek with his knuckles. "You have nothing to be sorry about. At every moment when I should have swept you into my arms, I've panicked and pushed you away."

Charlotte lifted her eyes and shook her head. "You can't take all the blame."

"My God, woman! Will you not let me win just this once?" His feigned frustration transformed into a grin.

She threw her hands up in the air. "All right. You win. You're a bastard! Now let's have dinner."

Perhaps it was relief or the respite from anguish

over their impending parting, but they spent the evening as if things were normal. They talked into the night until, at some point, they grew silent.

"I suppose I should go." He gave her shoulder a squeeze and leaned forward, preparing to stand.

"Ian, part of me wants you to stay."

His eyes crinkled. "That's my favorite part of you."

She smiled and let out a sigh. "It would just make it harder."

He lifted an eyebrow. "I can't argue with that."

She shut her eyes. "I have got to get better at choosing my words." She lifted her eyes. "Don't get me wrong. There is nothing I want more at this moment."

His face brightened.

She looked down at her hands. "Which is why it's... well, it's just a bad idea for so many reasons."

"I can't think of one."

Charlotte's face wrinkled as she closed her eyes. When she was able to open them and look into his, she was honest and open. "It would hurt that much more to leave you."

Ian said nothing. All they could share was the truth, and there were no more words to express it. He kissed her. That kiss broke her heart, and she couldn't even tell him how much.

TEN

IAN LEANED over the breakfast table. "I wish you'd let me drive you to the airport."

She shook her head and caught sight of Robby and Ivy. If it were possible to look as sad as Charlotte felt at that moment, those two did. God, she loved the Scots—those two in particular. "Ian, I can't. I mean, you can't. I'll need the entire length of the drive for the ugly cry I've got planned."

He gripped her hand. "Charlotte."

"Ian. Look at us—we've got the name thing down." She flashed a weak smile, but it dissolved.

All the wishes and thoughts they could no longer express hung between them. There was nothing left to do but stare with abandon as unexpressed longing and regret clouded their eyes. Maybe at some point in the future, Charlotte would reflect on the moment for the honest expression of love that it was. It would take her a very long time to get to that point.

She took a deep breath, set down her napkin, and stood. Ian folded his hand about hers, and they walked silently to the car parked outside the front door. He wrapped his arms around her, and they clung to each other while Robby put Charlotte's bags in the car.

The rear car door closed as if sounding a knell. Ian kissed her and pressed his cheek to hers. He let go and took a step back.

A cold breeze shocked Charlotte's senses as she turned and got into the car. Ian closed the door, and they stared at one another, their faces devoid of expression except for the pain in their eyes.

Robby got in and drove down the drive then pulled onto the road.

Snow seemed to be flying horizontally at the windshield. "Robby, that's a lot of snow."

"There's a storm on the way."

"I think it's arrived."

"Aye."

He drove on in silence over roads that were coated and slick.

Charlotte pulled out her phone to check the flight status. "Ugh. Nothing. When do you think I might get a signal?"

"At the airport."

"You're kidding."

He didn't have the face of a guy who was kidding. "Sorry."

The snow grew deeper until they were driving through several inches of slush. Charlotte stopped wondering about the flight status and began to worry about making it to the airport.

Robby's eyes were fixed straight ahead. He seemed like a good driver. He'd handled a couple of skids well, certainly better than Charlotte would have. Still, she wished she'd taken Ian up on his offer to drive her to the airport. If she'd made the wrong call, it wouldn't have been her first on the trip.

Her first mistake had been falling in love. There, she'd said it—thought it. And then she'd tried to pretend that it wasn't what it so obviously was.

The car went into a spin, pulling Charlotte back to her dangerous reality. Robby cursed as he fought to recover. They spun around and came to a stop well off the road. All was quiet except for the hum of the motor and the relentless back-and-forth rhythm of the windshield wipers.

"Bollocks!" Robby stared straight ahead for a moment. "Are you okay?"

"Yeah, I'm okay. How 'bout you?"

"Aye."

"This isn't just your warm-hearted Scottish hospitality talking? You're really okay?"

"Aye, Miss Glass."

"Robby." She shook her head slightly. "What have I told you to call me?"

"Charlotte."

"Good. I'd hate to think we met our demise before arriving at a first-name basis."

"Aye, Miss—I mean Charlotte." He tried to pull onto the road again, but all he managed to do was spin the tires.

"I think you're supposed to rock the car back and forth," Charlotte said.

Robby glimpsed in the rearview mirror. "Look behind us."

They were stuck facing the road. Charlotte glanced back and gasped. They were no more than a couple of feet from the edge of a cliff. She turned around and pressed her back to the car seat.

Robby tried several more times to pull forward but just dug them in deeper.

"Robby, stop."

"We can't just sit here."

"Turn off the car."

Robby did so then turned to her, looking puzzled.

Charlotte said, "Do you smell that? I think the

exhaust pipe must be jammed with snow. The exhaust has nowhere to go but in here."

Robby tried to open the window. Nothing happened, then he shook his head, turned the key, and the windows went down. Snow blew in, but so did fresh air.

"I'll see if I can unblock the exhaust." He got out of the car and was gone for a minute before he returned. "It's too close to the edge. We're on a bit of a slope. I don't think the car's going anywhere, but I might. Between the wind and the snow, it's too risky."

With the car fully aired out, Robby rolled up the windows.

Charlotte pulled out her phone. "Please let there be a signal." She dialed 999. Nothing happened. A few curse words came out of her mouth.

"The coverage up here is patchy," Robby said, explaining the obvious.

"It's okay. We'll get through this." If she said it, it might become true. Charlotte opened a texting window. If a call wouldn't go through, maybe a text would. Then she realized that she'd never had to call Ian.

"Robby, do you have Ian's mobile number?"

He took out his phone and gave it to her. She thumb-typed, *"Please send help. Skidded off road and got stuck."*

As she texted, she asked, "Do you think it'll go through?"

Robby turned to face her. "Honestly?"

Charlotte nodded.

He hesitated then shook his head slowly. "No." He turned on the car's hazard lights. When he looked at her crestfallen expression, he added, "But it might. I'll text Ivy too. Ian has a habit of leaving his phone about, but Ivy always has hers."

Charlotte feigned being insulted. "Ian? So he gets the first-name treatment, but I'm 'Miss Glass'?"

Robby grinned. "I've known him forever."

She smiled and looked through the few bare spots on the windows that weren't covered with snow. "So how well do you know this area?"

"I grew up here."

"Fantastic! Where's the nearest place we might find shelter?"

"Craigthorn."

"Great." She smirked as she looked out the window. Nothing had changed; all she saw was blowing snow. "Okay. So what's next?"

"We wait."

"What? We can't just sit here and accept it. We can't be that far from the castle. We could walk it."

"We are not going to walk."

"Says who?"

Robby turned to face her. "Says I. We're safest right here."

"You're awfully bossy."

A shy smile bloomed on his face. "Aye, that's what Ivy says."

"Oh? I hadn't noticed you being bossy."

"Not at work. I try to be professional in front of the guests."

Charlotte's eyes narrowed. "So you and Ivy..."

"We're engaged."

"Oh!" They did make an adorable couple. "That's... so sweet."

"That's what we said about you and Ian," he said with a mischievous spark in his eye.

Charlotte's eyes opened wide. "Oh. Well, I guess you couldn't help but notice."

"Don't worry. We like you with him."

"Why, thank you!" She pretended to fluff up her hair. "I'll bet you say that to all the girlfriends."

He shook his head vehemently. "Oh no. Not the last one. We didn't like her at all."

Charlotte was all ears, but she felt guilty about it. It didn't feel right to be badmouthing the ex while she and Robby were in danger of freezing to death. So with amazing restraint, she simply said, "Oh."

"She made Ivy cry the first time we met her."

"What?" Charlotte was already outraged. "Ivy is so nice. How could anyone do that to her?"

"Aye. Ivy was serving tea to her in the breakfast room."

Charlotte tried not to think too much about why Phoebe might have been there for breakfast. She could have been in the neighborhood and stopped by... first thing in the morning. Things like that happened.

Robby went on with his story. "Poor Ivy. She'd only been there for a week. She was so nervous, the cup rattled, and she spilled it right on Miss Forsythe's lap."

"Oh no!"

"Oh, aye! Ian jumped up to get a napkin from a nearby table. While he was gone, she grabbed Ivy's arm, pulled her close, and said, 'You stupid cunt. That's how people get sacked.' Poor Ivy just took it, but when she walked away, she had tears in her eyes."

"Poor thing!"

Robby's eyes narrowed. "And that cow was all smiles by the time Ian came back, so he never knew what a terrible person Miss Forsythe was."

"Wow." Charlotte couldn't imagine how that must have been for Ivy.

"So, no, we don't like her. And yes, we like you."

Charlotte shivered and rubbed her arms.

"Och, where's my head?" He climbed halfway over

the seat and returned with a couple of blankets and two bottles of water.

"Whose idea was that?"

He grinned. "Ian's. They're for guests during outings and car crashes."

"Perfect." She took a drink. Being a proper New Yorker, she was always thinking ahead to where she would take her next bathroom break. At home, she had the public restrooms mapped out in her mind so she would never have to walk more than ten blocks to relieve herself. She looked through the window and saw yellow snow in her future.

She and Robby wrapped themselves in the blankets and waited.

"So, Robby, how did you and Ivy meet?"

They spent the next hour talking, but as snow accumulated about the car, Charlotte couldn't hold the thought back. "Someone should get here soon, right?"

After a long silence, Robby said, "Right." But he didn't sound convinced.

IAN STOOD UP. He'd been watching the news. All the flights out of Scotland were cancelled. Every airport was closed. A weather system had changed course and was bearing down on the Highlands.

He went down the hallway and stuck his head in the door of the staff room. The manager rushed past, mumbling about some pressing issue with the kitchen staff. Ian spied Ivy in the corner, taking her lunch break. "If you hear from Robby, let me know."

She looked up, concerned. "Why? What's happened?"

"Nothing that I know of, but he should have been back by now."

She glanced at her watch. "Oh! I got busy and lost track of the time." Her eyes widened. "They left over two hours ago!"

"Never mind," Ian said. "Get your coat on. Grab some blankets. Oh, bollocks! He's driving my car."

Ivy was already on her way out of the room. "We can take mine."

"Look up hypothermia and take few screenshots to read on the road in case we don't have a mobile signal."

Two minutes later, they pulled onto the road that led to the airport.

Ian had insisted on driving. "Read everything you downloaded. If they haven't come back, they're stuck somewhere in the car. With any luck, they'll have enough gas to keep the car warm." For Ivy's sake, he tried to sound calm and optimistic, but he felt in his gut that something was wrong.

The world looked gray and bleak. Plows had been

through, leaving rows of deep snow on both sides of the road. Ian was worried he and Ivy might not be able to see the Rover. If Robby and Charlotte had swerved off the road, they could be completely out of sight. He didn't tell Ivy, but he was acutely aware of any signs of tire tracks on long stretches of road that ran beside the steep cliffs. *Hang on, Charlotte. I'm coming.*

Ian hated himself for ever letting Robby drive to the airport—not that Ian could have changed whatever might have happened, but at least he would have been with Charlotte. He tamped down the desperate emotions that would only serve to get in the way.

"Ian, look!"

The tire tracks were almost filled in by new snowfall, but the tracks led them to the faint flashing of lights that shone through the snow.

"Good eye, Ivy!" Ian pulled over as close as he could to the Rover. Then he got out, grabbed a shovel, and climbed through the snow to the car. He brushed snow from the passenger window and tapped on it. When he got no response, he started to shovel. Ivy did the same on the driver's side. Ian tapped his shovel handle against the window. When there was no response from inside, he decided to break in through the back window. The back one would be safer.

On the other side of the car, Robby opened his

window a crack and called out to Ian. Ivy rushed over to his side of the car.

"Unlock the doors!" Ian shouted.

CHARLOTTE DREAMED she was walking through snow, wearing boots, a long scarf that waved in the wind, and nothing else. There was nothing but snow in every direction. Someone was clapping. She kept trying to walk away, but the clapping wouldn't stop. *Clap. Clap. Clap.*

"Charlotte!"

Someone shook her. She wished they would just leave her alone. Someone kept shouting her name. *How annoying!* She gave up, opened her eyes, and looked down. "Clothes. Wow, that's a relief." Then she lifted her eyes to find Ian staring down at her.

"Come on, lass. Let's get you home."

She looked about, puzzled. "I guess I took a nap. I'm so cold."

"Aye, I'm taking you home, where it's warm."

"But the airport..."

"The flights are all grounded because of the storm."

Ian helped Charlotte to the car, but Robby insisted he didn't need help. Ivy stayed close by Robby until he and Charlotte were safely seated inside the car.

Ivy read from her phone and lifted Robby's then Charlotte's wrists. "Check their pulses. If they're not normal, we'll need to get them to a hospital. I'll take their temperatures on the way. Ian, would you wrap the blankets around their torsos? Don't do the extremities yet."

With that done, Ivy checked temperatures while Ian pulled Charlotte's luggage out of the Rover and put it in the back of the car. Then they headed for home.

ELEVEN

An hour later, Robby and Charlotte were seated by the fire with their legs propped up and covered with blankets. Ivy had moved her chair close to Robby's. As they sipped hot tea, Ian paced and spoke quietly on his phone in the adjoining room to the laird's room. When he was finished, he returned, pulled a chair next to Charlotte's, and sat.

"I've got good news and bad news." He glanced at each of them. "The good news is—"

Charlotte interrupted him. "Wait. Don't we get to pick which to hear first?"

"No," Ian said. "The good news is, I spoke with my doctor. He said if your vitals never got to the extreme range, and since they're normal now, you should be fine. But if you have any symptoms—"

"Such as?" Charlotte asked, worried.

"I was getting to that. Any confusion?"

Both Charlotte and Robby shook their heads.

"Good. Slow or shallow breathing?"

Once more, the answer was no.

The corner of Ian's mouth turned up. "Are either of you in a coma?"

Charlotte smirked. "Uh, no."

"Last one, and this is the tough one—well, it will be for me. If you start frantically ripping your clothes off—"

"Well, now you're just dreaming," Charlotte said.

Ian raised his right hand. "I swear it's a symptom."

They all stared at him, and he nodded. "Anyway, should that happen, we're not to take advantage of the situation." He glanced over at Ivy. "I believe the doctor might have meant that for me, specifically. Instead, should that happen, we should take you immediately to the hospital. That last part is real."

They all quieted down until Charlotte remembered what he'd said before. "What's the bad news?"

Ian took her hand. "It's rather good news for me, but for you... I'm sorry. The planes are grounded at least through tomorrow and probably through at least part of Christmas Day."

Charlotte looked into his eyes, unable to hide her

delight. "Two more days." Then she saddened. "But I'll miss Christmas with my family."

Ian covered her hand with his. "I'm sorry. We'll do our best to make up for it."

Although disappointed in part, Charlotte played down that emotion. "I'd better call home and let my mom know." She started to get up, but Ian stopped her.

"You're not going anywhere. Doctor's orders."

"I need my phone."

"Then I'll get it." On his way, he stopped before Ivy. "Robby shouldn't risk going out again in the cold. Would you mind seeing if we have a room available? He can stay here tonight." Ian's eyes twinkled. "And I imagine you'll have to stay, too, to keep an eye on his condition."

Robby winked at her, and Ivy's face turned beet red.

She got up. "I'll go make the arrangements."

With the other two gone, Charlotte turned to Robby. "Will Ivy be okay? I think Ian embarrassed her. If he's forced you two into an awkward situation, we could see about getting a second room."

He wrinkled his face. "Och, no. We've been together since high school, so... No. Ivy's shy where others are concerned. We'll be fine."

Before long, all the phone calls and arrangements

were made. Ivy and Robby headed off to their room, leaving Charlotte and Ian behind.

Ian leaned close and held Charlotte's hand in both of his. "I can't lie and say I'm not glad to have you here for another day, maybe two. But I truly am sorry you won't be with your family."

"I know. I've got mixed emotions myself."

"What can I do to make it feel more like home?"

Charlotte couldn't help but smile at the way Ian always thought about her comfort and her feelings. "You don't need to do a thing. The castle looks gorgeous. It's perfect. It's the people, you know? That's what I'll miss." She hadn't expected to get choked up at the thought. She waved her hand over her teary eyes. "Oh, wow. Look at me. I'm not usually like this. I blame the hypothermia." She avoided his eyes while she regained her composure.

He gave her hand a squeeze. "It's all right. Please don't censor yourself for my sake."

She lifted her eyes and gazed at him, full of wonder for how lucky she was just to know him. She had two more days. She didn't want thoughts of their impossible future to cloud the small window of time. Still, she had a nagging feeling that he was the one—that one great love that too few ever knew. This would be the great love of her life. And the greatest regret. Years in the future, she might sit, old and alone, on her porch, but at least she would know she had been loved. Knowing that, could love ever really be lost?

THEY STAYED up late and talked about Christmas and family. Charlotte was an only child. As she described her family and their holidays together, Ian found himself wishing he had what she did. They weren't perfect, but no family was. Yet what she described was a family that shared time at holiday gatherings with no expectations except simply being together.

Charlotte rested her chin on her hand. "Tell me about your Christmas memories."

"I was young when I lost my parents—my first year at boarding school. I have a few vague flashes of memory, like a dream you wake up from that wasn't finished. I mostly remember the feeling of home and the loss of it. When they were there, I was safe." Speaking about it brought memories he would not share with Charlotte. He took a breath and went on. "After the car accident, my life was at boarding school. On holidays, I was shuffled around among relatives. They all took their turn, did their duty."

"That sounds..." She looked too sad to voice her thoughts.

"It was." He slowly nodded then lifted his eyes to meet hers. "That's why I envy what you have."

A sudden determination filled Charlotte's face. "We'll have that. You know, there are no flights tomorrow, Christmas Eve. And even if I left the next day, I'd be traveling on Christmas and wouldn't get to my family in time. So why don't I reschedule my flight for the day after Christmas? Surely the airports will be open by then. And that gives us two days—my two favorite days of the year, I might add—and we'll be each other's family for those two days. We'll make up our own traditions, and it will be whatever we want it to be."

"I'd like that." He kissed her softly.

"One more thing," she said quietly.

He smiled and brushed strands of stray hair from her forehead. "Whatever you want."

"The whole way to the airport—well, technically not the whole way since we never actually made it, but..." She looked at him with shining eyes. "The thing is, I kept thinking that I... we..."

He lifted his eyebrows and leaned a bit forward in anticipation.

I want to sleep with you. Why is that such a hard thing to say? Because it wasn't the sleeping, it was the driving emotion behind it that complicated matters. She might let it slip that she loved him. Then what? He might be appalled. Good thing he wasn't wearing a tie, or he probably would have loosened it due to the awkward discomfort she was causing. Still, he had to have feelings for her. No one could kiss like that without feeling something. And oh man, could he ever kiss. Her mind and her eyes wandered to his lips then to the rest of the features that so wildly appealed to her. This was crazy. She could sit here and dream about him, or she could do something about it.

"So, Ian, the thing is, I read a lot."

"Not a surprise since you're a librarian."

"Right. So, everything I've ever read—well, in the romance novels, anyway—says the best way to recover from hypothermia is from body heat."

He appeared to be trying to suppress a smile with little success. Then he drew his eyebrows together and looked almost serious. "Yes, well, I'm all for anything that helps you to recover, although according to the doctor, you should be recovered by now."

Charlotte wrinkled her face. "Yeah, I'm probably fine." She was so disappointed.

Ian moved closer. "But maybe I should check your body temperature, just to be safe."

She caught a faint whiff of his soap or cologne. Whatever it was, it smelled good, and she wanted to bury her face in that smell, so long as his body was part of the deal.

He circled his arms about her and whispered close to her ear. "So, tell me about this hypothermia cure."

Once she felt his warm breath in her ear, it was over. He had only himself to blame. "They have to get naked. For the body heat. It's purely medicinal."

He brushed his lips against hers. "If we must, then, for the sake of your well-being..."

"I'm pretty sure it would be great for my well-being."

He touched his lips to hers again and gave her a dizzying kiss, then he stood up and held out his hand. Charlotte took it, and he led her to the bedroom.

TWELVE

Charlotte opened her eyes. She reached over for Ian, but his side of the bed was empty. She sat up and found him in the sitting room, adding a log to the fire. She watched him and wondered how she could leave him. He was strong and confident, gentle and loving. Until then, she'd felt as though something had always been missing, but she'd buried that yearning and dismissed it as an unrealistic expectation then had proceeded to make the best of her life. But she hadn't been unrealistic. She just hadn't met Ian yet.

He climbed back into bed and propped himself up on his elbow. "So what's the plan for today?"

"Us."

"Good plan."

By the time they made it down to breakfast, it was closer to lunch. The regular breakfast service was over, but Ian told Charlotte he had some pull with the staff, so he headed off to the kitchen to scrounge up something to eat.

While he was gone, Charlotte texted an update to Jen then stared out the window with a ridiculous grin on her face, and she didn't even care. If anyone had asked her a week ago whether two people could feel like this after only a week, she would have told them they were naive dreamers who were setting themselves up for a fall.

But she realized now that life wasn't as predictable as she'd always known it to be. Life had moments of magic that could leave one breathless. Even if such moments were fleeting, they remained in a gallery of memories there to visit at will, on a whim, or in moments when one needed comfort the most. She would not take for granted her fleeting time with Ian.

He returned with a tray, and they quietly talked and gazed out at the sparkling blanket of snow.

Charlotte felt as if her heart might burst from contentment. "So, Ian..."

He mimicked her tone with a mischievous grin. "Yes, Charlotte?"

"What would make this the perfect Christmas Eve for you?"

"This."

She squinted. "Breakfast?"

"Aye, breakfast and lunch and supper and the times in between... with you." He kissed her palm and held it to his cheek.

"Oh, look!" Charlotte pointed outside, where Robby and Ivy were making a snowman, occasionally taking time out to throw snow at one another. She smiled. "They look so happy."

"Aye." He frowned. "Although I don't think that's the best post-hypothermia therapy."

She watched them wistfully. "I know, but remember when you felt young and invincible?"

"And you're such an old sage?"

"I'm twenty-seven."

He rolled his eyes and leaned back dramatically. "My God, you're a relic."

She shook her head, resigned. "Yeah, but I'm feisty." She furrowed her brow and regarded him. "How old are you?"

"Thirty-three."

"Yikes!" She sipped her coffee and watched for a moment as Robby and Ivy headed back to the castle. "So how is it you haven't..." Suddenly, it occurred to her that asking him why he hadn't been married was not the right topic for this otherwise perfect moment, so she searched for an alternative. "How is it you haven't... haven't"—she looked about and spied a Christmas tree in the corner—"haven't got a Christmas tree in the laird's room?" *Really? That's the best you could do?*

He looked at her strangely. "We've got a huge tree in the entrance hall, another in the breakfast room... let's see, and the dining room. And there's a small one in the library as well. Exactly how many trees do you need?"

She could see that he thought she'd gone mad, but it was too late to stop now. "And where do you put your presents?"

"Away."

"Away?"

"Yes. I open them, and then I put them away."

"You don't save them for Christmas?"

He avoided her stunned gaze. "Do you realize it's after noon? If we're going to make it to the village before the shops close, we'll have to leave soon."

That got Charlotte's attention. She wanted to get Ian something for Christmas. "Okay. I'll be ready in twenty minutes." She got up and headed for the exit.

Ian called after her. "Good. I'll be on the bench in the hallway, waiting for you."

Without slowing down, she called back, "Assuming you get there first."

TWENTY MINUTES LATER, Charlotte sat waiting on the bench as Ian walked down the stairs. She'd only just sat down, but she didn't share that with him. He was visibly taken aback.

Charlotte was not. "When I say twenty minutes, I mean twenty minutes."

"Duly noted. Impressive!"

Charlotte indulged in a self-satisfied smile.

They got into the Rover, which looked a bit worse for wear after having been towed to the castle. But other than some scrapes from some fencing she and Robby had apparently skidded through, it was in fine running order and would get them where they needed to go. Charlotte spent most of the drive trying to think of a gift to get Ian. She was not the best gift giver, and she wanted his gift to be special. Her usual gift card would simply not do.

They arrived one hour before the shops were all set to close, so Charlotte got down to business. She'd come up with an idea but needed to see if any shops in the village would have what she sought. There was only one gift shop in the village, so that dispensed with her hope of splitting up for some shopping. While Ian chatted with the male half of the couple that owned the shop, Charlotte pulled the wife off to the side and whispered, "Can you help me with a Christmas emergency?"

With their heads together, they worked out the details in a hushed conversation. It would take the woman a few minutes, but she thought she could manage it. Charlotte shopped slowly, stalling for time despite Ian's suggestions to move on. He indulged her for a while, but his patience ran out. He put his arm about Charlotte's waist and inched her toward the door.

Just when Charlotte thought all was lost, the female owner rushed over to her. "Would you like some shortbreads? I've put some samples in this bag for you." She pressed the small bag into Charlotte's hands.

Charlotte smiled warmly. "Thank you so much! You're too kind."

"Och, it's nothing. Happy Christmas!"

"Same to you."

As they left the warmth of the shop, they heard singing. "Oh, look, Ian!" A group of children were singing carols by the old mercat cross.

Ian put his arm about Charlotte's shoulders, and they headed that way. No longer preoccupied with her gift-buying task, she looked around at the holiday decorations and lights. The village would have been lovely enough on its own, but it looked especially charming and quaint all decked out for the holiday season. As the carolers finished a song, Charlotte shivered, so Ian insisted on ushering her into the pub for something to warm her. They chose a table close to the fire. Ian left Charlotte there while he went to the bar. He returned minutes later with a hot coffee drink.

"Oh, Irish coffee! That's perfect!"

Ian put on a thick Scottish accent. "Och, lass! Mind your tongue. You're in Scotland. I'll no' hear anymore o' tha' blether. Do ye ken what's in this cup? Scotch. And coffee. So it's called..."

She smiled patiently. "Scotch coffee?"

He nodded his approval. "Aye, there's a good lass."

The pub was lively with holiday cheer. Charlotte hooked her arm around Ian's and felt wholly content as she fell more and more deeply in love.

CHARLOTTE WAS STILL LAUGHING at something Ian had said as they rushed into the castle to get out of the cold. They headed upstairs. Ian agreed to drop Charlotte off at her room, provided she join him in the laird's room posthaste. She changed into a tunic and leggings, sent a quick text to Jen, and headed to Ian's suite of rooms.

There, they spent a quiet evening watching an old Christmas movie until their interest in the movie lost out to their interest in each another. As they walked to the bedroom, Charlotte said, "It's past midnight. That means it's no longer Christmas Eve. It's officially Christmas."

Ian swept her into his arms and kissed her. "Happy Christmas."

"Merry Christmas." This would be their last full day together.

The bright morning sun picked up the red in Charlotte's auburn curls as she sat cross-legged on the settee. Ian brought her a coffee and sat down beside her. She took a sip then sprang to her feet. "Wait right there." She returned with a small wrapped package and handed it to him.

Concern lined his face. "But I wasn't expecting anything."

"That's what makes it more fun. Relax, Ian. It's just a little something to remind you of me."

He opened it and looked at her. "A key fob?"

She couldn't hold back her smile. "Look at it closely."

"What's this on it?"

"My phone number. Turn it over."

He did as she directed.

"My email address." She looked up and shrugged. "Just in case."

He shook his head and smiled. "Very practical."

"Right? You're welcome."

He pulled her onto his lap. "How can I thank you?"

She felt suddenly serious. "By making use of it."

"I will."

"And don't lose it! I know how you are with your keys."

"Promise." He gazed deeply into her eyes. "Oh, by the way! Sorry, love, but I must ask you to move."

Charlotte returned to her side of the settee and took another drink of her coffee while Ian went to the bedroom. He returned shortly and handed a small package to her.

"When did you do this?"

"About the same time as you, but you were too busy to notice. Go ahead. Open it."

Inside, she found a silver charm bracelet with a single charm on it.

"It's a castle," he said.

"I can see that."

He grew suddenly wistful. "So you won't forget me. Although if you don't wear it, it's not going to help." He frowned. "I didn't really think this through well enough."

"I'll remember you—with or without a reminder." Mixed emotions of longing and the sadness of parting filled their gazes.

Ian broke the spell softly. "It's almost time for the Christmas buffet. I usually leave the public side of the business to the general manager, but I should make an appearance."

They dressed up and went downstairs, where they received paper crowns and crackers and joined in the festivities. As the laird, Ian was sought out for more than his share of conversation, which gave Charlotte a chance to sit back and observe him.

In a suit and tie, he looked handsome, although he looked equally appealing in a sweater and jeans. His hair was attractively tousled from the habit he had of combing his fingers through it—something she wanted to do at the moment. His gray eyes were gentle and thoughtful as he listened intently to whoever was talking. The candles and soft lighting cast a warm glow on the planes of his face. It was all she could do not to pull out her phone and take a picture. She wanted to remember it all—how he looked in the warmth of the room, the scent of fresh pine garlands, how it felt to be with him both there and alone, and everything else about Ian.

She wanted to remember the man she would never forget.

THE NEXT DAY, Charlotte sat in the business-class lounge with a glass of champagne and a collection of moist, crumpled cocktail napkins in her hand. She was facing the window so fewer people would see the tears that just reappeared when she wiped them away. Her phone beeped. Of course, the text was from Jen. Charlotte's best friend would not only worry about her but also know when to do it, adjusting for the time change.

Jen: *How are you?*

Charlotte replied quickly: *Fine. Can't talk now, what with the tears.*

Jen: *Oh, honey...*

Charlotte: *Yeah. It's not pretty. We'll talk soon.*

Jen: *K ((Hugs))*

She took a deep breath, wiped her eyes, and had another sip of champagne, just in case seven hours on an airplane wouldn't dehydrate her enough.

THIRTEEN

New Year's Eve found Jen scanning a book for a patron while Charlotte looked through a catalog for new books to order.

Jen watched the patron walk out of earshot and glanced over at Charlotte. "Remind me again why we're here on New Year's Eve."

"Job fulfillment. And money."

Jen lifted her chin toward a man walking into the library, clad in workout attire. She held her fist up like a microphone and quietly said, "It's 9:13. Shoeless Joe Jogger is running late. Will he make it in time? It's down to the wire. Here he goes, *New York Times* in hand, headband in pocket. He's sitting, shoes off, and... done. 9:15." She made a noise into her hands then said in a stage whisper, "And the crowd goes wild!" Several silent seconds passed. "Hello?"

Charlotte looked up. "I'm sorry. What?"

Jen gave her a pitying look. "Nothing."

Charlotte woke up from her daydream. "Oh, sorry. That was funny."

Jen smirked. "I could tell from your laughter."

A woman approached the desk, leaned close, and spoke in surreptitious tones. "There's a man with a sword outside of the entrance. He's waving it around."

"Sorry," Jen said. "He's kind of a regular. He likes to practice outside. We'll take care of it."

While the patron walked over to wait by the door, Jen opened a drawer. She and Charlotte each pulled out a pencil. Jen's was shorter, so she went to the door to keep patrons from going outside until the situation was resolved.

Charlotte reached for the phone and called the police. "Hello, this is Charlotte from the library. Samurai Swordsman is practicing outside our front door."

Almost immediately, two officers emerged from the police station next door and proceeded to speak with the swordsman. He sheathed his sword and handed it to them, then the officers escorted him to the station.

Jen returned to the desk. "I wish he'd find somewhere else to practice. He frightens the patrons, and he annoys me. Oh—and are you sure you don't have a secret stash of new number-two pencils in there?"

Charlotte smiled. "I can't help having superior skill."

"At drawing straws—I mean pencils?"

Charlotte smiled innocently.

Jen shook her head. "This isn't right. I want a referee."

Charlotte laughed and put a handful of books on the book cart.

When their turns at the circulation desk were over, they went into their shared office. Jen closed her computer window and rolled her chair closer to Charlotte's. "So, have you heard from Castle Man?"

Charlotte shook her head. "We've texted a couple of times. He hasn't been super demonstrative."

"That doesn't mean anything."

Charlotte sighed. "I know. He's kind of a buttoned-up guy, which is fine, but it makes it hard to know where we stand."

Jen squinted. "We? So this 'we' thing is ongoing?"

"I think so? It feels different, but that's to be expected. Right? You know how these things are."

Jen started to nod but then stopped. "Well, actually, no. I've never had one of these things. Why don't you tell me?" She leaned on Charlotte's desk, resting her elbows on the table and her chin in her hands.

Charlotte sighed. "I don't know. Maybe he felt obligated to reach out. I mean, I did give him a key fob with my email and phone number engraved on the back."

Jen suppressed a smirk. "Subtle. I like it."

Charlotte curled her lip at Jen's sarcasm. "It was better than my first plan—a surprise tattoo."

Jen's eyes sparkled. "The surprise part is always hard to pull off." She spied something and narrowed her eyes. "What's that on your wrist?"

Charlotte lifted her wrist and looked at her charm bracelet. Then she held out her wrist for Jen to examine the charm.

"Is this his castle?"

"No. It's just a regular castle. But he said he hoped it would remind me of him."

"Aw, that's so sweet!"

"Yeah, I know. So I should be happy, right? I met a wonderful guy, and we had a great time. That should be enough."

Jen furrowed her brow. "Not if you love him."

Charlotte exhaled. "Yeah."

"So you love him!"

"I didn't say that."

"I think you must have at some point. How else

would I know?" Jen smiled knowingly. "Look, I'm no expert. I mean, look at me. Thirty-one. Single. No prospects in sight. But I think the way love works is that if you both feel the same way, you find a way to be together."

"If."

Jen shook her head. "Look, I wasn't there, but it sounded to me like there was something very real going on between you two."

Charlotte grimaced. "Yeah. There was. But now that we're apart, it just seems so unreal. Ugh. Sorry to drag you into my middle-school angst."

Jen grinned. "Hey, sixth grade was a good year for me. New braces, bad haircut, glasses with tape on the left hinge. Seriously, Charlotte, call me crazy or corny, but I firmly believe that true love will not be denied."

AT 12:45 P.M., Jen was more than ready to leave. She leaned closer to Charlotte and spoke quietly. "Almost time. I've got the keys to lock up. New Year's Eve, here we come!"

"I'll make the announcement." Charlotte picked up the phone and started to speak over the public-address system as Jen headed for the main entrance. "Good afternoon. The library will be closing in fifteen minutes. If you have items to check out, please bring them to the circulation desk at this time. All copy machines, computers, and stack lights will be turned off at this time. We will reopen tomor—excuse me—the day after tomorrow at nine a.m. Have a good evening and a happy New Year."

Just before Jen reached the door, a tall, very good-looking man stepped inside.

"I'm sorry. We're closing." She was tempted to make an exception for him, based on good looks alone, but it was New Year's Eve. She and Charlotte had plans—not that plans couldn't be changed.

"I'm not here for a book. I'm looking for Charlotte Glass. I understand she's a librarian here."

Jen started to smile. Not many hot guys with a Scottish accent stopped by the library before closing. She narrowed her eyes at him. "What's your name?"

"Ian MacKay."

"Ian MacKay? From..."

"Scotland. Is Charlotte here?"

Jen grinned. "Yes, she is."

The relief that came over his face warmed Jen's heart, which was a pretty tall order. But then Ian was a pretty tall guy.

She motioned for him to follow her. "Come with me."

CHARLOTTE SCANNED the bar code of a chapter book then handed it to a girl who looked about eight years old. "I read that when I was your age, and I loved it. Let me know what you think."

The girl beamed, clutched the book to her chest, and left with her father.

Charlotte's thoughts filled with memories of the summer she read that whole series while visiting her grandparents. It was one of her happiest childhood memories.

In her peripheral vision, a movement caught her eye. She gasped and stared. Ian stood so still for a moment that she didn't think he was real. Then he strode toward her. Still stunned, Charlotte glanced around to make sure all the patrons were gone. The only person there was Jen, who stood in the doorway to the main entrance hallway with a huge smile on her face.

Charlotte hurried out from behind the desk and flung her arms about Ian. He held her and kissed her hair and her cheek. She kissed him then buried her face in his chest and breathed in. When she looked up, she found that warm gaze she loved even more than she had a week ago. She gripped his shoulders. "I can't believe it. You're here!"

"Aye. And you're here. I was worried that you might be closed. I don't know where you live."

She was still shaking her head. "You didn't tell me."

"I didn't know!"

"But—"

"I'll tell you all about it later."

Jen chimed in and hooked her arm about Ian's. "Good, 'cause we're closing. Then we're all going to begin phase one of our New Year's Eve celebration."

A look of concern came over Ian. "Oh, of course. You've got plans. I'm so sorry. Look, I can—"

"Come with us." Jen grinned. "It's been decided."

Charlotte smiled. Jen was the one who had orchestrated the entire New Year's Eve celebration. Charlotte would have loved to stay home with Ian, but she didn't want to bail on Jen. But now that Ian was there, she couldn't imagine a better way to ring in the new year.

Both Jen and Charlotte had come to work packed for the night, Jen from her Brooklyn apartment and Charlotte from Queens. Three months ago, they'd gotten together with a small group of friends and booked a New Year's Eve package in a theater district hotel, where they planned to watch the ball drop from the rooftop deck.

With two hours until check-in, they dropped off

their bags at the hotel then went out to wander in Midtown until check-in time. After inching in the opposite direction of Times Square, they made their way to Bryant Park, where they sat and regrouped.

Jen looked at her watch. "I've got an emergency manicure, so—"

"A what?" Charlotte wasn't buying that, but Jen gave her a look, so she didn't argue the point.

"So I'm going to have to leave you two without supervision." Jen gave them the sort of look Charlotte recalled getting from the teachers on overnight school field trips.

"I'll meet you back at the hotel." Jen winked and took off.

Charlotte turned to Ian, and they gazed at one another.

"I missed you," he said.

"I missed you too. For all five days since I left. Ian, how did you manage this?"

"It was all my friend Lewis's doing." Ian looked down as a bashful grin formed. "Evidently, I mentioned you once or twice after you left. I'm told I was quite tedious about it."

Charlotte tried not to look too pleased.

"An old schoolmate of ours had mentioned to Lewis that he'd chartered a plane to come here for the New Year. Of course, he was taking some family and friends. Lewis asked if he had one more seat, and he did. So here I am."

"For how long?"

"Until tomorrow."

"Tomorrow?" Charlotte tried to hide her disappointment, but she desperately wished it were longer. "It's more than I thought we'd have a few hours ago."

"And I'm all yours until then."

Charlotte held his face in her gloved hands and kissed him.

He said her name softly. "Let's go find someplace warm."

FOURTEEN

JEN WAS in the hotel lobby when they arrived to check in. "Before you say anything, it's a done deal. I'm staying in Katie and Tasha's room."

Charlotte took in a breath and began to protest.

"Nope. Not a word. Relax. There's a sofa bed. I'll be fine." She gave Charlotte a hug and whispered, "Happy New Year."

Jen left them and headed for the elevator while Charlotte checked in. When they got to their room, Charlotte locked the door and turned to Ian. "We've got an hour before we're due downstairs for cocktails." He felt so good in her arms. She had no intention of letting go, but he took a step back and held on to her shoulders.

"We need to talk."

Charlotte's heart sank. Nothing good ever came after those words.

He looked very intense. "I don't know why I didn't tell you before you left."

The blood drained from her face. "Oh, crap. You're married."

His eyebrows drew together as his jaw went slack. "I drop everything to come see you, and that's your first thought—that I'm married?"

"It's the best I could do on short notice."

He lowered his chin and looked into her eyes. "No. I'm not married."

Charlotte's eyes shut as she took in a deep breath and sighed with relief. "Okay, good. Good to know."

"Charlotte." He lifted her chin. "After you left, I guess that's when it hit me. I missed you."

"Yeah, but did you cry at the airport?"

"Well, no. But I was driving. You cried?"

"I created a used-tissue sculpture."

He smiled.

"In the interest of public health, I had to dispose of it," she added.

"I'm not nearly so artistic, but I did realize something."

"I think I need to sit down." Her head was spinning. That look in his eyes went straight to her heart and points beyond. She nearly begged him to stop looking at her that way, but she didn't want him to.

He seemed worried. "Are you all right?"

She sat down on the edge of the bed. "Yes. I'm just... You're here, and I... I'm so—"

He sat down beside her and took her hands in his. "Charlotte, I love you."

She felt as though she wanted to cry. Or fling herself at him. Maybe jump up and down. But she couldn't seem to move.

He looked a bit worried. "Have I... Have I said something wrong?"

"No!" Charlotte lowered her voice. "No. Sorry for shouting. I love you too." She exhaled with relief. "We love us. Each other, I mean."

"We do," he whispered as he kissed her.

"Did you just tell me you—"

He kissed her again. "Yes."

"Have I fallen asleep? Am I dreaming?"

"No," he said softly. "Come here." He opened his arms and enveloped her in them.

THEY WERE a few minutes late for dinner, but Jen, Tasha, and Katie didn't seem to mind. Throughout the first course, Ian patiently endured being interrogated by Charlotte's friends before the conversation turned to other things—like celebrating. After dinner, they went to a comedy club then returned to the hotel in even better spirits. They stepped off the elevator and onto the rooftop deck, which sported a bar, a DJ, and a spectacular view of Times Square. The time came to count down, and they watched the ball drop. Ian swept her into his arms for a kiss, and they sang "Auld Lang Syne." Charlotte had never been moved by the song like she was in that moment. She was so deeply in love with this man who was leaving the next day.

THE NEXT MORNING, they were quiet and close, as if the enchantment would end if they weren't careful. Charlotte didn't feel sad yet. It felt more as if they'd passed the point of needing words and needed only each other.

After brunch, Charlotte walked Ian out to the curb while her friends waited at the door. His friend's limo was waiting, so they only had time for a quick embrace before he got into the car and rode away to the airport. Her friends joined her at the curb, and Jen gave her hand a squeeze. Then they all headed for the Forty-Second Street subway station.

While her friends chatted and laughed, Charlotte

walked through Times Square in silence. It had been swept and cleaned up as if nothing had happened mere hours before, which made her feel as though Ian's visit could have been a dream. It had gone by so fast, but one thing made it more real.

Ian had told her he loved her.

FIFTEEN

CHARLOTTE'S PHONE rang at four in the morning. She reached over and pressed the alarm clock button—one of two, plus her phone—all set to make sure she got to work no matter what. On the third ring, she opened her eyes and grabbed her phone from the nightstand.

"Hello?"

"Charlotte, it's Ian."

She sat up and groggily ran her hand through her hair. "Is something wrong?"

"No. Oh God, sorry. It must be early there."

"That's okay." She yawned. "How are you?"

"I should call back later."

"No, I'll be at work. Talk to me. I like the sound of your voice."

"Charlotte, I can't stop thinking of you."

"Me too—I mean about you. Never mind. It's too early."

"I know it's too soon to make any sort of plans together, assuming you'd ever want to. I'm getting ahead of myself. Do you ever think of the future? With me, I mean."

"Well..." She hesitated to reveal her feelings. "Yes."

"Me too." He hastened to add, "It's too soon. I know. We barely know each other. And I have some matters I've got to resolve before... or first, rather."

Charlotte sat up straighter and tried to clear her head.

Ian continued. "As you can probably guess, I've put some thought into this. It's a long plane ride home." He chuckled, but it sounded nervous and a little forced. "This next part may sound a bit mad, but I thought we might consider a sort of arrangement."

"Arrangement?"

"There's an old tradition in Scotland called handfasting. I was thinking of trying our own version of it. It's sort of a test, but not of you or of me. It's a test of time, I suppose—of the feelings we share."

"Ian, I'm barely awake. This sounds serious."

"All I ask is that you think about it. I don't need an answer now. I'm not suggesting anything formal like an engagement. We've barely just met. Having met your friends, I know they'd be ready to talk you down from that limb, and rightly so. Mine too."

"Ian, I..." She didn't know what to say. Of course she'd thought about marriage, but not in real, down-to-earth terms. He was right. It was too soon, and she was half asleep.

"It would be just between us. But if we both feel the same way in a year and a day..." He paused and cleared his throat. "What was I thinking? I should've done this in person, but I miss you, and I don't know when I'll see you again. I want us to see if we can make this work."

She rubbed her face and her eyes. "Okay."

"What I'm trying to say is, there would be no obligation. All I'd ask is that if you found somebody else, you'd tell me."

"Okay."

"If we can overcome the long distance between us, and we both feel the same way in a year and a day, would you marry me then?"

"That sounds an awful lot like an engagement."

"Aye, but without a formal announcement. You could back out at any time."

"So could you."

"Charlotte."

How can he send chills through me by just saying my name?

He went on. "I wouldn't want to. I just don't want to put you under that kind of pressure. And the truth is, I'm not in a position to offer you any more than my heart at the moment. But I love you, and I don't want to lose you."

Charlotte began to wonder if she were, in fact, dreaming. "Ian, don't take this the wrong way, but can I have that in writing?"

For a moment, he was silent. "Are you joking?"

"No, seriously, I'm not a morning person. You've known that from the start. I'm not sure I'm even awake, and I haven't had any coffee. I can't make a life-changing decision before coffee."

"Right. I'll send it later today. Just say you'll consider it."

"I will."

"Charlotte, I love you. Now go back to sleep."

"I love you too." She pressed the button to end the call and muttered, "Handfasting?"

She lay down and pulled the covers back over her shoulders.

THE LIBRARY WAS busy all morning. Charlotte said goodbye to the last of the nannies and packed up the props from her Toddler Tune Time program. As she carried her tub of props and supplies past the children's room circulation desk, Jen glanced up while checking out a patron. "Don't you dare leave without me."

"Oh, don't worry."

Minutes later, they walked out onto the street. "What the hell, Charlotte?" Jen blurted out. "You don't just drop a bomb like that and go on with your morning."

"I know. I just—I can't believe it."

By the time they sat down for lunch in a nearby sandwich shop, Charlotte had brought Jen up to speed on Ian's phone call.

"So a sort of engagement without the commitment?" Jen made a face and shook her head.

Charlotte nodded. "I know. It sounds weird. But I don't think he meant it that way."

"What way?"

"The way that made you scrunch up your face when I told you." She took a sip from her water bottle.

Jen was still frowning. "I'm trying to understand. Is it, like, a Scottish thing? They don't believe in engagements?"

Charlotte couldn't help but laugh lightly. "No. They pretty much get engaged and get married like regular people."

Jen looked straight at Charlotte. "Except Ian."

Jen was making it worse. Charlotte felt more confused than her friend did. "I guess. I don't know."

Jen shook her head. "I think those are the words of a commitment-phobe. An extremely good-looking and amiable one, but still..."

"Amiable? Oh, I'd say he's a bit more than that."

"Okay, he's smart and interesting."

"And amazing, exciting, extremely attractive..."

"And afraid to commit. Who proposes by phone in the middle of the night?"

"It wasn't a proposal."

"Exactly." Jen softened the blow with a pitiful pout.

Charlotte sighed.

BACK AT WORK, Charlotte spent every spare minute mulling over the concerns Jen had raised. She couldn't blame Jen for not understanding when she didn't, either. If Jen had come to her with a similar story, she would have reacted the same way. Part of her thought love was clouding her otherwise good sense. Yet she couldn't believe Ian would hurt her. But how well did she really know him?

Jen asked her out for a drink after work, no doubt

because she could see how troubled Charlotte was. But Charlotte made an excuse and headed for home.

On the way home, Charlotte stopped at a deli and ordered a sandwich to take home for dinner. As she continued toward home, she spied the Christmas shop where she'd bought her castle ornament. To her disappointment, the gift shop was closed.

She went closer, shaded her eyes, and peered through the dusty windows. It looked as though it had been abandoned for months. The entire store was empty except for the counter and a few collapsing shelves on the wall. A box and a small pile of trash lay in the center of the old wooden floor. She looked up at the sign. It was gone. *That was quick.* Just a week ago, it had been open, but the dust and debris appeared older than that. Charlotte decided that she must have the wrong block.

She turned to continue on her way and almost tripped over an old homeless man. "I'm so sorry! Are you okay?"

He looked up at her with knowing eyes. "Don't worry. I'm fine."

Something about him seemed familiar, but she dismissed the thought. The poor man was so thin and frail. "Are you hungry?" Charlotte reached into her bag, pulled out her deli sandwich, and gave it to him.

"Thank you. You're very kind. A lot of people forget us after the holidays."

She didn't feel very kind. She would have just walked past him, lost in thoughts of herself, if she hadn't literally run into him. She took out some loose bills from her pocket. "This could buy you some breakfast tomorrow."

He looked surprised as he thanked her.

"Take care of yourself."

He nodded. "You too. *Carpe diem.*"

She started to walk away then squinted and looked back, but the man was too busy unwrapping the sandwich to notice. On her way down the stairs to the subway, her phone vibrated. She pulled it out and saw a new text. Her heart did a somersault. It was from Ian.

"Charlotte, per your request, it's too much for a text message. Check your email."

A sinking feeling in her gut overwhelmed her. No, she couldn't do it. She could not read his email on the subway. If she was going to lose it, she would rather do it at home.

CHARLOTTE CLOSED her door and sat down at the table. But there was no email. She checked to see if Ian had texted again, but there was nothing there, either.

She heaved a sigh and got up to get something out of the freezer to microwave for dinner.

The phone rang, and she answered it without looking at the screen.

"Charlotte?"

"Ian. I thought—"

"I know. But I can't do it."

She didn't know how to respond.

Before she could, Ian said, "I tried writing it down. It was worse."

"Okay. Talk to me. I didn't really mean it literally, I don't think. I mean, I don't know what I said. I was half-asleep."

"It's all right. I just want you to know that I meant what I said. I love you, and I want to find a way to make this work."

Charlotte sighed. "I do too, but—"

"Good. That's a start."

"I said 'but.'"

"I ignored it."

Charlotte grinned in spite of herself. "I know."

"Charlotte, my love, I'm asking for a year and a day. If we can't work things out by then, we'll give up. But I think we should, you know, seize the day."

"*Carpe diem,*" Charlotte muttered to herself.

"Charlotte?"

That was what the old man had said. She looked

up and sighed. Could they actually make this work? All she knew was that she wanted to try. "Okay."

"Okay? You'll give me a chance?"

"Yes."

He exhaled with a sound of such relief that Charlotte wanted to throw her arms about him right then and kiss him.

"Ian, maybe we could get together in... a month?"

"Yes. We could alternate visits."

"Yeah, I can try to get a cheap flight to Inverness."

"Yes. Let's plan on it. Send me your itinerary as soon as you've booked it."

"When would be good for you?"

"Whenever it is, if I've got plans, I'll cancel them."

Charlotte grinned at hearing his enthusiasm. "Okay."

His tone grew serious. "A month will be good."

Charlotte disagreed. "A month is forever."

"Aye, love, but you need time to think about this. I want you to be sure it's what you want—that I'm who you want."

"Same for you."

"No, I already know."

Charlotte couldn't seem to breathe, let alone give voice to her feelings. She managed an inadequate "Okay." Her heart was so full, but her head was just spinning. Maybe Ian was right. She needed to be able to think things through calmly and make a well-reasoned decision. At the moment, all she could think of was how much she wished she could feel his lips on hers and his body against hers.

"Well, I'll let you go," Ian said. "Good night, Charlotte."

"Good night."

Charlotte set down the phone. She didn't know how a long-distance relationship could work. But she had to try.

SIXTEEN

ONE MONTH Later

Charlotte straightened up her desk and put away the stray pens she'd managed to accumulate over the course of the day. She put her bag crosswise over her shoulder, rested her hand on the handle of her carry-on bag, and stared at the wall clock with keen eyes.

"Oh, go on," the children's room director said.

Charlotte felt guilty. "But it's ten minutes early."

"That clock must be wrong. I've got five o'clock." She called out, "How 'bout you, Jen?"

Jen stuck her head in the door and grinned. "Five o'clock."

Charlotte's eyes lit up. "Well, okay." She took a deep breath and exhaled. Jen squeezed her hand as she passed, and then she was off—on her way to the airport to catch an overnight flight to Scotland.

It didn't seem quite real. She was going to see him. They'd talked daily—long talks about every possible topic. She'd even introduced him to her parents via video chat while spending a weekend at home. Her father thought the separation was probably good for the relationship. That way, they could get to know each other without any distractions. She'd stifled a laugh at the time. Oh, how she missed those distractions!

She arrived at the airport and waited in line. She was flying economy this time, but she didn't care. She could cope with taking only carry-on luggage and bringing her own takeout meal on the plane. She didn't need in-flight entertainment. But when she found herself in a middle seat between two armrest hogs, she regretted not having paid extra for seat reservations. There was nothing to do except pull out her neck pillow and eye mask and hope she could sleep through most of the flight.

Unfortunately, that was the only dream she had that night.

Now sleep-deprived, she waited through long lines at customs and immigration. Ian texted that he was waiting on the other side of the doors. It took all of her self-control to keep from storming the exit.

When it was her turn, the officer seemed to ask more questions than usual. But he finally got to the last one. "Have you anything to declare?"

She was so sleep-deprived and so eager to see Ian that she had a sudden urge to answer, "Yeah, I declare this is taking too long!" But she summoned her last ounce of good sense and refrained.

At last, she walked through the doors to a sea of faces. She didn't see Ian, so she kept walking.

"Charlotte!"

She turned. For an instant, they froze, their eyes locked. Then he swept her into his arms and lifted her off the floor while he clutched her against him. Time stopped. Nothing else mattered.

By the time he set her down, her head was spinning from the sheer joy of being together. They soaked in the sight of one another, then he took her face in his hands and kissed her. His lips brushed her forehead as he whispered, "You're here."

"It's been such a long month," Charlotte said softly.

Ian squeezed her in his arms again. "Let's get out of here." He carried her bag as they walked arm in arm to the Rover, with its familiar scraped bumper from the snowstorm mishap.

"Just as I remembered it."

Ian opened the passenger door for Charlotte, put her bag in the back, and drove off.

When they pulled up to Craigthorn, Ivy and Robby were there to greet them. They all walked in, laughing and talking, and Charlotte felt as if she'd come home.

Ian set down her bag and closed the door to the laird's room. "I hope you don't mind, but you're staying with me this time." He smiled and looked down at her. "I'm glad that you're here."

Charlotte was too. On the flight over, she'd had a nagging fear that it wouldn't feel the same. The holidays could be a magical time, but she was afraid that after a month apart, their feelings might have changed. But when she looked into his eyes, the same powerful pull was still there. And that was the end of the talking.

CHARLOTTE WOKE up in the late afternoon, alone. "Ian?"

"In here." He appeared in the doorway. "I didn't want to disturb you. You seemed pretty tired."

Her eyes opened wide. "Did I fall asleep during..."

He laughed. "No. You had the good manners to wait, for the most part. Although my ego's a bit bruised. At one point, I had to splash water on your face to revive you."

"What?"

He grinned.

Now fully awake, she remembered—and well. There was no way she would have slept through that. She narrowed her eyes. "You're teasing me."

He leaned against the doorframe. "Aye, just a bit."

The sight of him took her breath away.

"Are you hungry?"

"Maybe. I'm not even sure." She looked at him frankly. "I don't think I do jet lag very well."

"How 'bout a walk? The cold air will bring you around. Then we'll have something to eat."

"Perfect."

THE WEEK PASSED in sheer bliss. They were closer than ever. When Charlotte would catch Ian staring at her, she was certain that he felt the same as she did. The ordinary things they did, like taking walks, making plans over meals, sharing thoughts in the late hours together—and the nights—it was all so perfect. Everything they did was a fresh, new discovery because they were doing it together. And Charlotte was happy. She wasn't even terribly sad when she thought of their parting because there was the underlying sense that they would be there for each other no matter what happened, and that wouldn't change.

The day before Charlotte was due to go home, a car pulled into the driveway just as Ian and Charlotte were coming back from a walk.

"Charlotte, you remember Lewis Pritchard, don't you?"

"Yes, I do. Nice to see you again, Lewis."

They shook hands, then Ian turned to Charlotte. "Lewis and I have a few business matters to go over." Apparently he noticed her confusion. "Lewis is my friend first, but he's also my accountant."

"Oh." As they walked inside, Charlotte was plagued by an uneasy feeling. Something about this meeting did not quite feel right, but Charlotte couldn't put her finger on it. It wasn't just Ian. Lewis looked abstracted as well. He hadn't just stopped randomly by to have Ian sign a few papers. And Ian wouldn't have scheduled something so routine on Charlotte's last day. He was far too thoughtful not to wait until after she was gone. Whatever it was, Charlotte decided it would be better to ignore it. It did not concern her. "I'll go see Ivy about some coffee. Would you like me to have some sent up? Or some tea?"

"Tea would be lovely. Thanks," Lewis said.

"Tea for me as well," Ian said.

Charlotte sat in the breakfast room and chatted with Ivy for a bit, but the girl soon went back to her job duties. Robby walked through once on his way to do something outside. Everyone in the castle had something to do. She finished her coffee and decided to go to the library to pay a visit to Walter Scott's *Lady of Lammermoor*.

Two hours later, she set down the book. "Well, things didn't go too well for them." She leaned back and looked at the floor-to-ceiling bookcases. She tried to imagine possessing all of these books—books that rarely got touched. Perhaps that was a good thing, as far as their condition was concerned. But there was something kind of wonderful about a public library filled with books that got used and worn out. The more worn they were, the more lives they had touched. It was why she had chosen her profession. Even so, sitting there all alone in the midst of all these magnificent books was the closest she would ever get to magic—that and being with Ian. She smiled to herself.

Robby opened the door. "There you are. Ian's been looking for you."

Charlotte thought she detected an urgent edge to his tone. "Where is he now?"

"He walked Mr. Pritchard out to his car, but he asked me to tell you to meet him in the laird's room."

"Okay. Thanks, Robby."

He smiled then bounded out the door and back down the hall.

SEVENTEEN

"There you are!" Ian smiled as Charlotte walked into the laird's room.

He seemed perfectly fine. Charlotte decided she'd been overthinking again. Her emotions were getting the better of her. Maybe this was how it would be. Trying to concentrate a month's worth of relationship into one week was an impossible task. Every small thing was magnified, every word, every lift of the eyebrow. It was good to realize those things, so she could throttle back her analytical and imaginative mind—a dangerous combination.

Ian walked into the bedroom. "I'm just going to throw on a fresh shirt, and then what would you say about stopping by the pub for a pint and some pub grub? Unless you'd like something more formal for supper?"

"No, that sounds fine." Charlotte walked to the window and looked out at the sea. The Christmas snow had melted while she was gone. Everything was gray except for the white foam on the tips of the water that lapped at the rocky shoreline. Overhead, swaths of translucent white streaked the pale sky. That combined with Craigthorn's near isolation made the place feel cold and a little bit lonely. But going home the next day shouldn't dampen the moment. She had one more night with Ian, and she was determined to enjoy it.

They drove into the village in near silence. "So, how's Lewis?"

"He's fine. Same old Lewis."

Charlotte nodded. "So he's an accountant?"

"He is."

"And you two went to school together?"

Ian answered in clipped words. "Yes, Charlotte. Anything else?"

Charlotte was stunned. "No." She stared out the window for the last few minutes of the drive.

Ian parked but didn't turn off the engine. He shifted to face her. "This was a bad idea."

"What?" He could have meant anything from coming to the village to her coming to Scotland. At the moment, she had no idea which.

"Do you mind?" he asked. "Let's go home. We've

missed supper, but we can scrounge something up from the kitchen."

"Sure." She tried not to frown as she stared out the window. Darkness had fallen, so she couldn't even try to read Ian's expression anymore.

When they got back, Ian paused at the foot of the stairs. "You go on up. I'll see if I can't find us something to eat."

At that point, Charlotte wasn't sure she was hungry, but she didn't want to raise another issue since nothing seemed to please him tonight. She went upstairs and left him to his dark mood.

THEY ATE their supper in relative silence. When they were both finished, Charlotte said, "I'll just take these dishes downstairs."

"Leave them. We need to talk." Ian's face was void of emotion.

"Okay." She eyed him, no longer searching for clues. From the feeling in the pit of her stomach, she didn't want to know what was bothering him.

His eyebrows drew together as he looked straight ahead, to the side, anywhere but at her. At long last, he said, "I'm sorry. This is hard to say."

"Have I done something to upset you?"

He turned to her, appearing stunned, and quickly said, "No!"

She exhaled, relieved. "Then what is it?"

He ran his hand through his hair. "I'm not very good at opening up." His eyes darted toward her, but he never made eye contact. "I suppose it all started at school. And then my parents... anyway, it's just always been easier to keep things to myself."

"Is it because I was asking about Lewis and school?"

"What? No." He shook his head. "No. Something's happened."

"It's obviously upset you. What can I do?"

He met her eyes, and in that moment, she caught just a glimpse of the pain he was grappling with. "It's so like you to say something like that."

"Anyone would. I can see you're in pain."

He took in a ragged breath. "You've done nothing wrong. None of this is your fault. It's absolutely all me. I've been struggling with something for a very long time. When I met you, I knew that it hadn't gone away, but I... I just wanted it to. Because I wanted you."

"Ian, I don't understand."

"I know. I'm not making sense." He took a deep breath and exhaled then looked straight at her. "The situation's gotten worse, and it's not going to work."

"Situation?" Her heart sank. "Ian, are you sick?"

"No. It's nothing like that."

She knew he wasn't purposely trying to torture her. She could see he was tortured enough for the two of them. She thought through each conversation they'd had, each word, in search of a clue. When she'd asked, he hadn't wanted to talk about it. But Lewis's visit seemed to have prompted his latest dark mood. Desperately searching, she wondered if what troubled him was connected to Lewis. She said gently, "Ian, are you gay?"

He almost smiled as he looked into her eyes. "No. I thought I'd made that quite clear."

She shrugged. "Okay. But you're obviously upset, and I'm apparently not good at guessing. Just tell me."

"Right." He nodded as though convincing himself. "Sorry. It's not easy to admit to. I'm sure my parents thought they'd left me well provided for. As an only child, I inherited everything—this castle and land and their wealth. It was all in a trust, with my uncle as trustee. Evidently, while I was at school, he was spending my money. He had a heart attack before he could spend all of it." He leaned his head back and rested it against the chair. "I've spent years trying to undo the damage. I thought one day I might. But it seems now as though I never will."

"Ian, you're not alone. We'll get through this."

His expression hardened. "No. We won't. Not together."

She couldn't speak. He could not be saying that.

"Craigthorn Castle has been in my family for generations, centuries. I'm the last of the line. You've seen the portrait gallery. It's like they're all looking down as I lose everything that they'd guarded so dearly."

She couldn't process any more. Her head was reeling.

Ian nodded. "A few years ago, I mortgaged Craigthorn to pay off back taxes. Not long after, I started the hotel business. You can't imagine what it costs to keep a centuries-old castle in good repair. For some years, I've been steadily falling behind. Now I've run out of options."

"I'm so sorry. I can't imagine what you must be going through."

"When I was sent off to school, I had a rough go of it for a while. But I learned how to manage." He turned to face her with that same hardened, expressionless face she'd seen earlier. "I won't put you through this. I've got to do this alone."

Charlotte shut her eyes. She wanted to be someplace else, anyplace where this wasn't happening, a place where her heart wasn't breaking. Then something snapped. "It's not fair." She turned to him.

"This isn't fair." A sudden surge of anger coursed through her. She stood up and paced. "You are not going to do this."

He watched her as she walked back and forth. "Charlotte, I'm sorry."

"Yeah, you're sorry. And you know what else? You love me. I only know that because you told me, like, a few dozen times this past week." She stopped and faced him, hands on hips.

"That was before I got the bank's letter."

"So all it took was a piece of paper to destroy your love for me?"

He stood up and faced her. "I know what you're trying to do. Let me save you the trouble. I'll admit it. I love you. I always will."

She acted as though that were news. "Really?"

His eyes softened. "Yes. But that doesn't change anything."

"Maybe not, but this will. I love you. And I'm not going anywhere—and I don't mean figuratively. So do what you want, but I'm calling the library, and I'm giving my notice. Then we're going to figure this out."

"Charlotte, no."

"Ian, yes. And want to know what else? I'm going to marry you." She could hardly bear to see the conflicting emotions in his eyes. But she took hold of his shoulders and met his troubled gaze. "Because I love you. And the only way you'll get rid of me is if you say you don't love me. Say you don't want to marry me. Do that, and I'll get on that plane and never trouble you again."

He shut his eyes and took in a breath then looked anywhere but at her.

Charlotte wasn't sure how long she could stave off the tears, but she steeled herself enough to say, "I mean it. Say you don't love me."

"I can't marry you." Ian turned and stormed out of the room.

EIGHTEEN

Ian sat in a booth in the corner of the pub—Charlotte's favorite booth—halfway through pint number two. Lewis walked in, got a pint from the bar, and sat down facing Ian. "Bloody hell, Ian!"

He looked up blankly.

Lewis glared at him. "One cryptic text? 'I can't do this.' With no explanation? I don't know if you're talking about giving up golf or your life." He cursed Ian a few times for good measure then took a drink of his beer and leaned back. He exhaled then spoke calmly. "So I take it we're not talking about your putting game."

Ian stared at the remnants of foam in his beer and shook his head. "No."

"So what is it? The money? Charlotte? You're sad because you don't get to see me enough?"

Ian looked up at Lewis, who managed to coax a smile from his friend. Then Ian muttered a curse, and they laughed. But it quickly faded.

"Two out of three."

"I'm obviously one. What's the other?" Lewis managed to keep a straight face.

Ian smirked, but a smile took its place. "You've always managed to make me laugh, even in the worst circumstances."

Lewis nodded. "It's a gift."

Ian took a drink then set down the glass and thought for a moment. "You know how I am. I don't share very well."

"I disagree. You're brilliant at a cocktail party. People adore you. You're witty and charming—"

"A learned skill."

Lewis continued. "As long as you're not talking about yourself."

"Precisely." Ian scanned the pub. People were scattered about in twos and threes, talking as though it were the easiest thing in the world. "People seem to like me, even Phoebe, who came just short of taking out full-page newspaper ads hinting at marriage. But she dropped me the minute she found out I was castle rich and cash poor."

Lewis gave a dismissive wave of his hand.

"Phoebe's a fool." A self-satisfied smile bloomed on his face. "Didn't I phrase that politely?"

"My point is, if anyone likes me, it's because I only let them see someone likable."

"Don't we all do that, really? We offer our best, and we do what we can to keep the worst secret."

Ian leaned forward on his elbows. "You've seen me at my worst."

"And I can say the same. And yet we're still friends."

"Because we were at school together. We hadn't yet learned to be guarded. I've since learned to keep people at a safe distance."

"Charlotte must love that about you."

Ian met Lewis's all-too-knowing gaze. His friend had an uncanny way of seeming so glib yet spotlighting the truth in the midst of it all.

"I told her about my finances."

Lewis raised an eyebrow. "Did you?"

"I told her because she had a right to know if we were going to be married."

Lewis eyed Ian intently.

"I can't make her go through it."

"I see. So..."

"She won't have to now. It's over. I'm freeing her of the burden."

"That's very magnanimous of you, sparing her like that."

"Yeah." Ian rubbed his forehead. "I wish I were that person. But as you well know, I'm sparing myself." He stared straight ahead, took a breath, and looked up. "My God, I'm eleven years old again, sitting on the edge of my bed." He took another deep breath, tamping down his emotions. "Sorry."

"Ah, don't apologize for being an exemplary student. We both learned very well how to bury the very thing that makes us human."

"I can't let her see me..."

"See you what?"

"Fall apart."

"And get up and keep going. She'll see that part, too, you know."

Ian glanced up. "I seriously doubt—"

"That she loves you?"

Ian was taken aback. "No, that she'd last long enough to see it."

"Same thing."

Ian averted his eyes from Lewis's judgment.

But Lewis wouldn't stop. "You're the one who wouldn't make it that far. Look at you. You've already given up, haven't you? Because you don't love her enough."

Ian's eyes burned with anger. "Don't be an ass. You don't know what I feel."

Lewis met Ian's anger calmly. "You're going to break her heart."

"Already have."

Lewis winced. "Because you're afraid to trust her."

The blow landed, and Ian had no retort.

"I know you feel safe in that cocoon you've spun 'round yourself," Lewis said. "Now look what you've done. You've got me speaking in analogies."

"Feel free to stop." Ian leaned back and finished his beer.

"I'll do that." Lewis turned and began to get up. "One last thing. If you don't open up and let someone love you, you'll wind up like me—alone." He got up and left.

Charlotte threw her scattered collection of tissues away and went out for a walk. It didn't last long. A cold wind blew off of the sea and chilled her until she sought the warmth of a fire. She wasn't sure where Ian was or whether she was ready to see him, so she thought she might hide out in the library. The guests would be downstairs for dinner, so she had at least a one-hour window to hide out, undisturbed.

She closed the door and sighed. The remaining embers of a fire glowed in the fireplace. She sank down into a comfy chair and shut her eyes for a moment. She'd made her grand stand. She still wondered where that had come from. Desperation, she supposed. But it hadn't done any good. He'd just stormed out and left her. Of course, he hadn't technically said he didn't love her as she had demanded. So by her rules, she should stay. But while he hadn't said he didn't love her, he'd demonstrated it well enough.

She was tired of thinking and even more tired of feeling. She would rest there for a while then go back to the room and start packing. She folded her legs up, hugged her knees to her chest, and surveyed the room. It was where she'd met Ian. She wondered if she hadn't fallen in love in that moment. There he'd sat, looking lordly and staggeringly handsome. What if she had just slept off her jet lag until morning? She might never have met him, at least not in that way. She might have been happier now but not as happy as she was with Ian.

She got up. Trying to rest was futile. She had to stop analyzing the incomprehensible. What she needed was to look at some books. Books never let her down. It wasn't as though she had access to many private collections like this. Nothing could make her forget Ian, but there was plenty in the library to distract her. She was drawn to one bookcase in the corner. It was high up and out of reach. She moved the rolling ladder over and climbed up. The glass cabinet door was stuck, but after working at it, she got it open. She'd just picked up a volume when the library door flew open. She twisted around to see who it was.

In a fury, Ian strode in and toward her. He grasped hold of her waist and lifted her down from the ladder.

"Ian!" She reached over to a nearby cabinet and set down the book she'd been holding while keeping her eyes locked on his.

Emotion burned in his eyes. Whether it was anger or passion, she wasn't quite sure. Until he pulled her into his arms and pressed his lips against hers. Then she knew. How she managed to stand after the kiss he gave her... well, she didn't know.

"Dammit, Charlotte, I love you!"

She held back, resisting her first impulse to throw her arms about his neck. "Are you sure? Because—"

"I was always sure. But I knew I couldn't be the man I wanted to be for you."

She gripped his shoulders. "What about the man I want you to be?"

He looked down and shrugged. "I don't know who that is. I just didn't want to fail you."

She shook his shoulders. "You are the man I want you to be. You're the man I want."

He looked at her in disbelief. "You don't know the real me. I'm losing Craigthorn. I can't even afford to fix my damn car."

She tossed her palms up and let her arms drop. "I don't care about that. I love you. Not your car. Not your castle." Her eyes sparkled. "Well, I can't lie. I do love Craigthorn, but it's not why I love you."

He smoothed his hands over her hair and searched her eyes. "Are you sure? It won't be easy."

"So I gathered," she said frankly.

"By the time this is over, I may have nothing left."

Tears stung her eyes. "You'll have me. And my love. That's all I've got, but it's yours."

NINETEEN

One Month Later

Lewis waited at the curb to drive Ian and Charlotte home from the airport. As they drove out of the airport, Lewis said, "Welcome home. Charlotte, Ian tells me you had a whirlwind month together in New York."

"We did. I trained my replacement, moved out of my apartment, sold my furniture to some tenants in my building, and now here I am."

"With only two suitcases? You travel light."

Charlotte laughed. "I'm having some boxes shipped over, and the rest is in storage."

"I see. And your family? How are they?"

"They're in love with Ian."

"Really? Now that is surprising." He gave Charlotte a wink.

Ian reached up from the back seat and gave Lewis a swat.

"Careful. I'm driving."

"You'll get to meet them when they come over for the wedding," Charlotte said. She looked back at Ian and smiled.

Lewis caught them up on his life and the local news. Charlotte noticed he left out anything having to do with Craigthorn Castle.

It wasn't until they'd arrived home and were comfortably ensconced in the sitting room chairs that Lewis broached the subject. "I've news from your solicitor. He met with the bank."

No one spoke for a moment.

"Yes, you said something on the phone about a stay of execution," Ian said.

The corner of Lewis's mouth turned up. "A time order, yes. They've agreed to lower the interest on the loan you took out on Craigthorn and to draw up a workable payment schedule."

Charlotte recognized Ian's look of forced calm. His face lost expression. He still reacted with apparent interest, but he was somehow removed.

"What good does a payment schedule do if I haven't the money for the payments?"

Lewis nodded. "I'm getting to that." He looked Ian straight in the eye and spoke softly. "It's contingent upon your agreeing to sell off some of your assets."

"Assets? You mean things that have been in my family for hundreds of years?"

"They believe that's your only chance of paying them off." He added softly, "I agree."

Ian rubbed his forehead and temples. "I can't."

Charlotte put her hand on Ian's. She had never seen Lewis look so grim.

Lewis waited a moment. "The thing is, if you don't sell some of it, you'll lose all of it. Ian, it's your best chance."

"I need time to think."

Lewis nodded. "Take all the time you need— between now and eleven a.m. tomorrow."

Ian cast a sharp look at him but said nothing.

Lewis got up to go. "This is not what anyone wants, but it happens, and people get through it. You will too."

Ian walked Lewis to the door.

THE NEXT MORNING, Ian went to the bank, and Charlotte underwent her usual battle with jet lag. When she awoke, it was lunchtime. While she ruminated on Ian's financial situation, something Lewis had said came to mind. There was no way around it. Ian would have to agree to sell off some assets. She thought of the things that might fetch some money at auction. The paintings, of course, and some items of furniture were bound to be worth something. How much, she didn't know. She finished her lunch and went for a walk through Craigthorn in search of ideas. Of course, Lewis would arrange for an appraiser to walk through and make recommendations, but Charlotte had to do something. Even if it didn't help, she would try.

She walked through the gallery, but she had no idea of the paintings' value. She would have to leave their assessment to the experts. She sighed. That would be true of more or less everything in the castle.

Except books.

Charlotte quickly went to the library. There were some beautiful volumes in there. She recalled one in particular that she'd started to look at. She smiled. It was the night Ian had come back to her. She glanced around at the shelves and reflected. In the few weeks since then, so much had happened.

That's nice, Charlotte. Now back to the books. Where was that small book with the gorgeous red leather-tooled cover? She climbed up on the ladder and looked inside the case where she'd found it, but it wasn't there. She tried all the shelves near it, then the tables and cabinet surfaces. Finding the book was becoming a personal mission. She wouldn't be content until she found it.

Charlotte tracked down Ivy. "Has anyone on the housekeeping staff found a book?" She described it.

"I don't know, but I'll ask."

The unmistakable sound of the closing front door sounded. Charlotte excused herself and left Ivy. She found Ian slowly climbing the stairs with the posture of a defeated man. Charlotte caught up to him and slipped her hand into his. Once inside the laird's room, he took off his tie and sat on the sofa by the window. Charlotte sat next to him. He didn't talk, but he squeezed her hand when she touched his.

After staring for some time at the ceiling, he said, "There are children starving all over the world, people living in desperate conditions, and here I am feeling sorry for myself. I'm such a prat."

"It's your home. And if I know you at all, this is not about losing this building or the things in it."

"I was so young when I lost my parents. I have so few memories. But I distinctly remember how it felt to come home."

Charlotte clasped Ian's hand. "It's that feeling of family—a sense of one's place in the past and the future, and most of all, love. That's what home is. That's what all people value—most of us, anyway. How many people trace back their family roots? It's something we naturally long for, a desire to belong to something greater. Why should you be any different?"

He turned and gazed into her eyes. "Thank you for that. I've been a bit of a wreck all morning."

"Understandably." She leaned her head on his shoulder.

"Sorry. I'll be fine. I just need a few minutes."

"I think you've been 'fine' for a very long time. Maybe it's time you just let yourself feel what you feel."

Ian sank into Charlotte's arms and wept.

THE DAYS that followed were a blur of difficult tasks, but they had to be done. Compiling the items going to auction was harder than moving because so much of what they sorted and packed would never be seen again—at least not by them. The auction appraisers had come through and identified items that might fetch a good price. Afterward, Ian and Charlotte sat down with Lewis and his spreadsheet and tallied up the potential results.

Lewis leaned back in his chair and stared at the screen. "There's always a chance for a pleasant surprise, but realistically speaking, this auction will buy you six months of debt payments, taxes, and building maintenance and repairs."

Ian perused the spreadsheet. "Okay."

But it wasn't okay. While it was a reprieve, six months would pass quickly.

Lewis turned to Ian. "Spring is coming. The hotel business will pick up. I'll make some calls. Maybe we can get a travel magazine spread. Let's see what we can do to fill up this place. And think about some promotions. You could offer a golf package with rounds here and on other nearby courses."

Ian narrowed his eyes. "The course needs some work, but the idea has merit."

Charlotte's mood brightened. "As we get more guests in, we can eventually reinvest, adding rooms. I can think of a half dozen rooms off the top of my head that we could fix up without too much of an investment. More rooms would mean more income."

The three brainstormed together and came up with some ideas to make finances stretch. Another auction would be inevitable. With the most valuable pieces gone, the resulting revenue would not last as long. But if they could gradually grow the hotel business income while reducing the cash outflow, they had hope of reversing their financial situation.

That night, Lewis stayed for supper, and they all went out to the pub to celebrate their new plans.

They'd had a few pints when Ian turned to Charlotte and spontaneously announced, "Let's get married!"

Charlotte laughed through her frown. "That's the plan. Remember our handfasting agreement?"

Ian waved his hand dismissively. "Screw the plan! Why wait for a year and a day? You're here. Why shack up with me when I can make an honest woman of you?"

She looked at Ian and couldn't help but smile. "I feel pretty honest right now."

Lewis leaned toward Charlotte, grinning. "Welcome to 1950."

Ian either didn't hear him or decided to ignore his friend. "We are not going to wait for a year and a day."

Charlotte gave Ian's shoulder a pat. "We can talk about it when you're a bit more clearheaded."

Ian took exception. "I don't have to be sober to know what I want."

Lewis laughed. "You might have to be sober to get it."

APPARENTLY, Ian was right. He knew just what he wanted. The next morning, after his headache subsided, they went to the registry office and published the banns.

As they walked out into a rare sunny February day, Ian put his arm around Charlotte's shoulders. "I told you I know what I want."

She grinned. "I like that about you."

Fifteen days later, The Much Honored Ian Donald MacKay, Laird of Craigthorn, and Charlotte Anne Glass were married in the great hall-turned-dining-room with Charlotte's parents and their friends Jen and Lewis looking on.

Afterward, as they sipped champagne, Jen came over to Charlotte. "I suppose you'll want me to address you from now on as Lady of Craigthorn."

Charlotte chuckled. "Yes, if you would."

Ian leaned over to Charlotte. "Don't get too attached. The title goes with the castle."

"Oh, I'm not giving that up. As the great Scottish philosopher, Yogi MacBerra, once said, 'It ain't over till it's over.'"

TWENTY

Auction day was almost there, and Charlotte was packing for London. "Ian, I'm missing one of my pearl earrings. Have you seen it?"

He adjusted his tie in the mirror. "No, I don't think so. Could you wear another pair?"

"No. These are my lucky earrings. They've never failed me." She'd worn them the night before, so she retraced her steps to the library. She and Ian had gone there for a nightcap to toast for good luck at auction.

As they had finished their whisky and set down their glasses, Ian spontaneously pinned her against a cabinet, kissed her senseless, and began to explore her thigh.

"Ian, the guests could come in!"

His warm breath brushed her ear as he whispered, "Then we'd better put on a good show."

She'd managed to steer him back to the privacy of the laird's room after that.

So the library was the first place she went searching. After a thorough search of the area, nothing turned up. There was space behind the cabinet where an earring might have fallen, but she would have to move it to search. It took some effort. They didn't make furniture like that anymore—solid and heavy—but she managed to move it a couple of inches. She pulled out her phone and shined the flashlight app into the dark space by the wall. *There it is!* Her lucky earring—and it lay on top of the book she'd searched for weeks ago.

There was no mistaking it. She'd been around books all her life, but that red leather-tooled cover was different from anything she'd ever seen, which was why she'd sought to have it appraised in the first place. Even if Ian didn't want to sell it, she was eager to satisfy her acute curiosity.

It fit in her hand like a mass-market paperback. She hadn't opened it yet, so the first thing she did was look inside. Charlotte gasped. "I probably shouldn't even be touching this with my bare hands." But she'd come that far; she couldn't resist. So she gently turned one page then the next. The book was beautifully scripted by hand. She didn't know Latin except to recognize it when she saw it. She stopped and carefully closed it. "Someone's got to see this."

She ran upstairs. "Ian?" She walked into the laird's room, where Ian sat, packed and waiting for her. "Tell me about this book."

He shrugged. "I don't know. I don't recall ever seeing it."

"It's from your library. Would you mind if we took it to London to have it appraised? I thought we might see if they could include it in the auction."

"I don't think they can just toss it up on the block like that," he said as he carried their bags to the door.

Charlotte wrinkled her nose. "Okay, but would it be all right if we had someone look at it?"

"With all that we're selling, what's one book?"

Charlotte took that as a yes. She slipped it inside a gift bag she'd saved from the wedding and tucked it between the folded garments in her suitcase.

After spending the night in a Bloomsbury boutique hotel, they arrived at the auction house the next morning. The place was a bustle of activity as the auction approached, but Charlotte would not be deterred. She wasted no time in asking the woman who greeted them if there were an appraiser available.

The woman seemed reluctant, so Charlotte lifted the gift bag and pulled out the book.

The woman's eyes narrowed. "May I see it?" She turned it over, examining the elaborately tooled front and back. She looked closely at the spine and the binding then opened it. Her eyes widened, and she lifted intense eyes. "Come with me."

Ten minutes later, the book was on a table. White gloves had been donned, and a handful of men and women looked like children on Christmas morning. By that time, Charlotte had told them everything she and Ian knew about the book, which wasn't much.

Finally, a gentleman who appeared to be the auction house's book appraisal expert approached them.

"Is there any chance of including it in the auction today?" Charlotte asked.

He looked horrified, as if she'd threatened his firstborn. "Oh, madam. I'm afraid that's out of the question. With your permission, we'd like to examine this further. I'd like to bring someone in from the British Library, as well as some others for verification."

"Really?" Charlotte turned to Ian, who appeared just as surprised.

The appraiser strongly stressed that they couldn't be sure yet, but there was a chance the book might be from the Monkwearmouth–Jarrow Abbey. He looked at her as if she should know what that meant.

He narrowed his questioning eyes. "St. Cuthbert's Gospel?"

Having no clue, Charlotte winced as she lifted her shoulders.

"Well..." He looked over his glasses. "We, here, all agree that this book was probably made by the same hands that made the St. Cuthbert Gospel, a book very much like this—in all likelihood, the same scribe. There are indications that it may even slightly predate the St. Cuthbert."

"Which would be when?" Charlotte asked.

"The early eighth century."

"Wow." Charlotte looked at Ian, who took the information in stride.

"Indeed," the appraiser said. "You might be interested to know that the St. Cuthbert Gospel last sold to the British Library for nine million pounds."

"What?" It was Ian's turn to be shocked.

Charlotte murmured her own calculation. "So in dollars, that would be..."

Before she could finish, the appraiser said, "Close to twelve million American dollars." He smiled to see they both finally appreciated what a find the book was. The man continued to explain. "Of course, the St. Cuthbert Gospel was found buried with a famous saint, which naturally enhances its value. So yours may not fetch quite as much as the St. Cuthbert. However, it is one of a very few Anglo-Saxon manuscripts to survive to this day, and that nine-million-pound sale was in 2012, so I'm quite optimistic that this could do nearly as well."

He excused himself to go gather some papers they would need to sign, giving the auction house permission to further examine the book. As he walked away, Charlotte turned her attention to her husband. "Ian, do you know what this means?"

Still in shock, Ian shook his head slowly. "Charlotte..."

She cleared her throat. "That's Lady of Craigthorn, if you please."

His eyes shone. "You can be Lady of whatever you want!" Then he lifted her into his arms and spun her around.

As he set her down, love for Ian eclipsed her excitement. "I just want to be Lady of wherever you are."

They kissed like nobody was watching.

"There you are!" Lewis said, coming to join them. "Sorry I'm late. Did I miss anything?"

ACKNOWLEDGMENTS

Thanks to Andrew Ziem, creator of Bleachbit, for graciously granting permission to mention his product.

As always, many thanks to Red Adept Editing.

THANK YOU!

Thank you, reader. With so many options, I appreciate your choosing my book to read. Your opinion matters, so please consider sharing a review to help other readers.

ALSO BY J.L. JARVIS

For a Reader's Guide to more books by J.L. Jarvis,

visit jljarvis.com/books.

BOOK NEWS

Would you like to know when the next book comes out? Sign up for book release news at:

news.jljarvis.com

ABOUT THE AUTHOR

J.L. Jarvis is a left-handed opera singer/teacher/lawyer who writes books. She received her undergraduate training from the University of Illinois at Urbana-Champaign and a doctorate from the University of Houston. She now lives and writes in New York.

Sign up to be notified of book releases and related news:
http://news.jljarvis.com

Follow JL online at:
Website: jljarvis.com
Facebook: facebook.jljarvis.com
Twitter: twitter.jljarvis.com
Tumblr: tumblr.jljarvis.com
Pinterest: pinterest.jljarvis.com
Bookbub: bookbub.jljarvis.com
Email: jl@jljarvis.com